Silver Strings

by

Adedoyin Ayeni

CHAPTER ONE

DARÀSIMI

My family all stood at the departure in the airport waiting with me before I boarded the plane as they all wanted to say their goodbyes before I left finally for New York. My sisters both stared at me with tears in their eyes and my mum trying her best to hold back hers .

They were my family and I was deeply going to miss them.

"Sister simì, don't forget us when you get there *o*. Make sure you make lots of money so you can send them to me" my youngest sister Tolu joked with a smile on her face making me tap her head softly.

"So you can spend them all on sweets and junk food *abi*?" I scolded with a smile

"No *joor*, maybe small *sha*" she teased making me laugh.

"You be a good girl and listen to mummy okay. I don't want to hear complaints over the phone while I'm there. You have to come out with the best results in your waec examinations"

"Before *nko*, don't you trust me again sis. You'll be shocked once I send you the results" she boasted proudly.

"It's okay *joor*, safe journey Dara. Make sure to call immediately you land" my other sister said with a straight face.

"I will, take care of mummy for me okay."

"I will" she replied with a smile pulling me for a hug before shortly releasing me.

"Mummy, don't stress yourself too much please. Make sure you eat your meals properly and rest when it is needed".

"I'll be fine simi, you just go there and succeed. You've already made me so proud already, your father would be really proud to see how much you've grown and how far you've come." She said mentioning about my dad making me feel emotional immediately.

"Thanks mum, I'm really going to miss all of you" I said with slight tears in my eyes hugging my family tightly.

I was really going to miss them so much.

♪♪♪♪♪

The plane safely landed and I was walking out of the airport with my luggage in hand as I hailed down a taxi straight to NYU. I got a scholarship to do my masters in Food Engineering right immediately after my graduation. I couldn't waste any more time in Nigeria, taking the shot immediately. I got admitted into my dream school, my student and work visa was approved and my mum was able to get me a plane ticket. It wasn't easy, I never imagined in a million years that I'll ever get to school in NYU but I decided to just take that one shot and out of five hundred international student applicants I was chosen and I couldn't be any more thankful.

The traffic was crazy and I was indeed surprised that it was real just like in the movies. Stuck in traffic for a while, I unlocked my phone scrolling through my application one more time still in awe that I was really here. I was one step close to fulfilling the dream my dad wanted.

NYU was his dream university. He wanted to pursue his musical career but could never fully achieve his dream. He did get in but sadly he was too poor to afford a plane ticket and that was the end to his dream.

Finally, I was here and I was going to do everything in my power to come out with the very best results. It was important for newly admitted graduate students to live on school campus so I made arrangements beforehand to stay in the school dormitory, hopefully my roommate was nice. The taxi dropped me inside the school's campus which was extremely large and I felt like a mice in a maze. Asking for directions towards the school dorms, I managed to pull my huge luggage with me as I tried locating it with the directions different people on campus gave me.

Finally reaching the dorms I went up to the reception office filling in the required paperwork and submitting the necessary information about me such as my medical records, admission status and printed receipts. Soon I was done with everything and she told me my room was on the fourth floor and with my small build I managed to pull my luggage up the stairs since the elevator was currently broken.

Knocking on the door with a slight pant the edge of my forehead building up a bit with beads of sweat. It was currently fall since I applied for September admittance and I was glad I didn't overthink and decided to put on something warm. My thoughts were cut off by the door opening and a girl about my age or younger stood right in front as she slowly accessed me. She was dark skinned with really exquisite facial features with her braids in a rough bun on top of her head. She had a very distinctive lip ring and I was slightly impressed by that.

"Hi, I'm your new roommate." Deciding to break the silence, her eyes left my worn out sneakers trudging back to my eyes and a hint of recognition flashed in them.

"You're daràsimi?" She asked in a very soft American accent.

"Yes, hi." I replied with a small smile hoping to come off as friendly.

"Hi, come in. I'll help you with your bags" she said making room for me and picking up my luggage as we both walked into the room.

I watched her place my luggage at the side of the room with an empty bed.

"That's yours. Welcome to NYU daràsimi" she beamed with a smile that made her tired looking eyes brighten.

"Thanks." I muttered feeling quite shy.

"I'm sure you must be really tired. It looks like you almost got lost on campus" she said giving me a sympathetic look making me feel very embarrassed.

"Yeah, didn't expect for the place to be this big."

"It's fine, you should take a nice shower. The bathroom is right there" she pointed to a small room in the far corner of our dorm room.

"Thanks, let me just call my family to let them know I've gotten here safely"

"Yeah sure, I have somewhere to be right now, so I'll give you space to settle right in. The empty part of the closet belongs to you." She explained pointing to the wardrobes as i admired her body structure.

She was tall and lean but it suited her and the way she rocked those yoga pants on a sleeveless top was so Bella Hadid coded.

"Oh okay, thank you." I stuttered immediately coming back to reality from the little trance she put me in.

She was really gorgeous and nice.

"Alright, I'll see you once I'm back" and with that

she left the room closing the door behind her leaving me with my thoughts and the silence as I looked around the room.

Our room was beautiful, the floors were wooden tiled and the walls were painted coral blue which gave off a warm vibe. Her side of the room was filled with posters of landmark places in the world.

She must love to travel.

Her bed side table was filled with so many pictures. Some with her friends, family and one with I think was her boyfriend because he had his lips on her cheek and she was grinning so happily.

I felt like a creep stalking her and I snapped myself back to reality deciding to just talk and get to know her instead.

Looking around my side of the room I noticed it was too plain and I decided to go shopping soon and get nice decorations to liven up the place a bit. Bringing out my phone from my purse I realized it was dead so I immediately plugged it in watching the screen come up.

Connecting to the dorm WiFi with the password I was given at the office I went straight to my WhatsApp contacts and immediately video calling my family. I sat on my bed raising my phone to my face close enough for all of them to see. Their faces filled with happy smiles as we all talked happily and I showed them my room and told them my roommate was okay. My mum prayed for me and wished the best for me. Once they were done talking to me I promised to always keep in touch.

Dropping my phone down finally to charge I pulled off my clothes taking out my bathroom supplies as I went in to take a nice long shower.

Once I was done showering I slipped on a nice pair of shorts and a crop top drying my wet hair with my blow dryer before finally settling down and sorting out my stuff. As I arranged my clothes neatly I noticed that she didn't really own that many clothes and mine was going to take a lot of room so I decided to leave some of mine in the bag only picking out the ones I'd actually wear.

Immediately I was done unpacking she busted in holding two plastic bags of McDonald's takeout.

"Hey, I see you're done unpacking" she said glancing towards the filled up closet.

"Yeah. Thanks for leaving me a lot of space, I kind of brought a lot of clothes"

"Oh it's fine, I don't really own that much clothes anyways." she said with a shrug.

"I actually didn't get your name though" I said shyly feeling embarrassed she knew my name and I didn't think to ask.

She opened the plastic bag as I watched her bring out a huge burger immediately taking a bite out of it.

"It's Dahlia" she answered

Wow, even her name sounded beautiful

"Are you a graduate student too?" I asked curiously.

"Yes I am and I am currently in my second year majoring in Geology and Archeology science." She explained as I looked at her in awe.

She must be extremely smart. Her course was intense. "Wow that's really cool. Mine is Food Engineering"

"Really? This is my very first time meeting an engineering student. Well then, it's really nice to meet you daràsimi" she said finding it a bit hard to pronounce my name.

"Just call me simì, it's easier and shorter that way" I politely offered with a smile.

"Okay cool, I like that simì"

I walked off to my bed picking up my phone and

decided to scroll through the internet and speak to some of my friends back home when she stood right in front of me holding one of the plastic bags and handing one over to me

"I figured out you might be really hungry. You must've had a long flight all the way from Nigeria. I got one for each of us. I hope it's okay" she offered with a smile making me feel really grateful for her kindness.

She was right. I was indeed hungry and was just too tired to get myself something to eat.

"Thank you dahlia."

"Just call me lia, most of my friends call me that." she offered politely with a smile.

"Okay lia."

This felt nice making a new friend.

"Oh before I forget. There's a party holding on downtown tonight for all fresher's. Wanna come with me? Instead of staying all alone tonight. It'll be nice you know to make some friends" she offered

"That's cool with me."

"Alright, when it's about time to go I'll let you know."

"Okay." I said smiling in satisfaction.

I can't wait.

CHAPTER TWO

DAMOLÀ

The smell of bleach was very overpowering as I opened the door to my office walking out towards the reception floor of the third level which I headed in the hospital.

Holding unto a file belonging to one of the patients and walking towards the nurses desk as they busied themselves with their work their eyes fully on their computer screens. I walked straight towards the head nurse, as I softly tapped my fingers on the desk immediately getting her attention as sat tall on her seat staring up at me.

"Doctor Damolà you could've rang for me instead

of coming all the way here" she offered her voice filled with a tinge of apology.

"It's fine, I noticed that Mr Newman's medical file was missing an MRI scan. I need it done as possible if he wants me to be able to locate where the tumor is in his body".

Dropping the file on her desk as I watched her go through it her eyes unable to find the scan results. She immediately closed it up muttering an apology and saying how she'll give him a call to come to the hospital as soon as possible for his scan.

"Do I have any more appointments tonight?" I asked straightforwardly.

"No sir you asked me to cancel all meetings for tonight."

"Good. Reschedule all of my surgeries for tomorrow and shift them to Thursday." I ordered

"Alright sir, but can I ask why? Because Doctor Rita already cleared out her schedule to assist you for tomor-row's surgery with Mr Tomlinson."

"I have something really important to do tomorrow so please just do as I say" I ordered rudely.

"Yes sir." she said quietly and with that I left the reception back to my office.

Entering my large office I sat back on my chair with the air conditioner cooling my tired face and making me a bit chilly. Feeling relaxed I stared up at the ceilings releasing a deep breath and softly twirling around on my seat as my mind slowly drifted to her. *My muse.*

It was a bit weird trying to imagine an eight year old girl with full black afro curls and a bubbly smile but she was the only person that ever made me happy. Growing up was a bit hard for me since I moved a lot as a child with my mother. I never knew who my father was neither do I have any vivid memories of him. I was born in New York but when I turned ten years old my mother moved us back to Nigeria and we stayed there for three years and during those years I met her and we grew up together and got really close to each other .

Bringing myself back to reality and refusing to keep on thinking about the past my mind slowly drifted to my mum as I greatly missed her. Tomorrow was her death anniversary. She died when I was fifteen from breast cancer. Just when things seemed to be getting better for the two of us I lost her and social workers took me in and for a while i was in the foster care system until I was old enough to live out on my own.

Picking up the only picture I had of her which was placed in a frame on the top my desk as I looked at her smiling face holding a little me close to her. My phone rang almost immediately the screen flashing with my best friend's name showing up. Picking it up and hearing his loud voice echoing loudly through the phone.

"Dami! Dude are you seriously not going to talk to me because I drank the wine in your kitchen cabinet??" He asked sounding incredulous at my current behavior lately.

"Yes" I answered curtly as I heard him sigh in slight annoyance.

"It was just one wine let it go already!" He snapped making the sides of my lip curl in amusement loving how much my attitude was ticking him off.

"No I won't. You went into my house unannounced and drank my favorite wine without my permission. That is unacceptable Tom" I spoke out in slight annoyance.

"Are you kidding me? We're best friends. That's what best friends do dumb fuck! When're you gonna let go of this your boundary issues" he shouted playfully over the phone.

"Maybe when you learn how to understand why

boundaries are put up and why I follow them" I said in a hard tone making him scoff playfully

"Oh please like I'd ever listen to you. A day's coming bro when those stupid boundaries you keep putting on will eventually fall and when that day comes I'll gladly laugh in your face and say I told you so"

"Why'd you call me?" I pushed ignoring his snide remark.

"Some kids at NYU are throwing a welcome party of some sort and they need someone to perform and I talked to them about you and played some of your songs and they liked it. So yeah they want you, you in?"

My lips quirked up in a small smile "Yeah I'm in, thanks"

"Of course. You're my bro. My ride or die." he teased lightly making me roll my eyes.

"Shut up."

"I'm sorry for drinking your wine though. I didn't realize it was your favorite" he apologized sincerely.

"It's okay, apology accepted"

"Alright, so I'll see you at the bar okay"

"Yeah, text me the address" I answered

"Oh and who knows Dami you might finally meet a girl that breaks those boundaries you keep putting up tonight" he added trying to sound mysterious.

"This is why you're single Tom. I'll see you at the bar tonight" and with that i hung up not waiting to hear what he had to say.

Tonight better be good.

♪♪♪♪♪

Tom and I sat in a corner at the rooftop bar observing the various students that came for the party with drinks in their hands as they mingled with one another enjoying the scenic view of the city. The air was chilly as I wrapped myself in my black leather jacket taking a shot of whisky the contents moving up to my brain and giving me that boost of confidence i needed to perform tonight.

"Damn, these college girls be looking extremely attractive tonight and making me miss school" he said checking out most of the ladies at the bar but I could care less.

A minute not less, two young girls walked up to us. One was dark skinned with long ginger colored braids and the other was white with brown hair and they both wore clothes that did nothing to hide their assets and I watched my best friend shamelessly drink in every inch of their bodies.

He was such a pig at times.

"Hi, do you guys attend NYU?" The dark skinned one said in a sultry voice her eyes on me as I felt her fingers prickle the skin on my shoulder as i lightly shoved it off.

Keeping quiet because i could care less who these girls were I turned my direction to my phone as my best friend carried on with the conversation.

"Nah but we were invited. My boy's playing tonight" I heard Tom say.

"Really? You play the guitar?" The white one chirped in excitement admiring my black acoustic guitar her eyes deeply swooning over my features.

I ignored her question refusing to join in on the conversation. I came here to perform not socialize with air headed college girls that didn't know the meaning of boundaries. My silence embarrassed her and I noticed the red rim on both sides of her cheeks. Tom immediately stepped in answering her question to make her feel less embarrassed than she was already.

"Yeah he's a singer"

"Wow double threat. Hot and talented" the dark skinned one said still in that annoying sultry voice, her hands not understanding personal space.

I pushed her arm off me giving her a look that made her recoil in slight embarrassment.

"Girls how about I make it up to you? Free drinks on me tonight. Yeah?" Tom offered brightly trying to lighten up their damp moods making them smile almost immediately. I watched him drag the both of them, his hands on both their hips to probably have fun with them before he turned to give me a "you could do better and what the hell is wrong with you?" look making me roll my eyes in slight annoyance.

I wasn't the type that socialized much and I pride myself in personal space and boundaries which those airheads couldn't seem to grasp. Adjusting the strap of my guitar, one of the organizers came up to me telling me how they need me up on stage to do my thing.

Picking up my guitar i took confident strides towards the stage as I watched people talk and mingle. At a corner I could see my best friend having the time of his life with the two airheads and I shook my head for him.

Adjusting the microphone about to start when I

noticed a full puff of black Afro curls at the entrance of the bar.

It couldn't be her there are lots of dark skinned girls in this party.

I removed my eyes from the entrance not getting a glimpse of her face as I softly tuned my guitar. Then closing my eyes I played the first chord. Deciding to start with a mellow slow song I imagined the tune in my head and let my fingers do their magic. Following up with the tune my mouth opened and I began to sing softly. The lyrics flowing out of me unable to stop as I enjoyed myself in my own little bubble.

Music was my life. It was something I deeply enjoyed and performing in front of people wasn't that much of a problem for me.

Slowly opening my eyes I noticed that most of the people had stopped what they were doing and all eyes were on me listening and watching me intently. I never needed an introduction you could say I was a shadow to my own self.

I loved to perform but I didn't want the attention and fame that came with it. I just want to play my music for people and help brighten their life in some special little way. I figured if music could help me through the darkest moments in my life it can for others to.

Raising my head to meet the eyes of everyone who watched me perform and not stopping with what I was doing my eyes locked with one I never thought I'd ever see again. She had grown up and she was in New York standing right in front of me staring up at me with a glint of adoration in her eyes. She obviously couldn't recognize me but I immediately recognized her. She had indeed matured over the years but those eyes never changed and that was when it hit me. My muse was back.

Immediately I was done performing I didn't even bother waiting to soak in the applause because I was off the stage looking for her. I needed to talk to her, I needed to see that she was real and I wasn't dreaming as usual. Finally noticing her among a group of people as she mingled with a smile on her face. I stood in a corner slowly accessing every little detail about her not in a hasty mood to approach her yet. She was petite with the right curves in all the right places as she relaxed her sides on the wall wearing jean shorts and a small corset top that clung to her like a second skin and on her small feet where leather black boots. She had tiny piercings on the sides of her ears and her face was completely free of makeup making her the most beautiful woman to me in this rooftop bar right now. She had full lips and a cute button nose and that black full Afro hair was put up in a tight puffy ponytail.

I was dying to talk to her, to inhale her scent and to hear her voice.

Slowly waiting for her to be done mingling I waited until she was all alone before approaching her. She stood leaning on the railings her eyes marveled by the view of New York City.

"It's beautiful." she whispered softly

"So are you."

Her eyes snapped off from the trance she was in searching for who said that only to land on me as i stood close to her loving how she smelled. She smelled nice, like vanilla and spice..

She seemed a bit struck as she stared at me in awe making me wonder if there was something on my face.

"Are you okay?" I asked politely

"Yeah, I'm good. I was just surprised to see you" she said and her voice was so smooth it amazed me.

"Why?" I asked because a part of me wondered if she still remembered me.

"Because it's my first night in New York and I never imagined a good looking guy like you approaching me especially one with a very impressive talent" she blurted out shyly making smile softly at that.

"It's your first night here?" I asked not wanting to accept her compliment. I honestly didn't think I was that good looking.

"Yes, I just moved all the way from Nigeria. Got a scholarship to do my masters in NYU" she explained.

"Really? That's very impressive"

"Thanks. what about you? Are you a student too?" She asked curiously

"No, I graduated a while back."

"Oh so what do you do now?"

I considered telling her I was a doctor and working as a highly trained surgical oncologist but I pushed it all to the back of my mind, the entire thing seeming too much to dump on her first night.

"Music. I perform at bars, clubs and open for concerts." I answered

"Really? That's so cool. I mean you're very talented

though" she complimented with a smile completely throwing me off at how good she looked with it.

"Thanks."

"I'm Daràsimi but you can call me simì" she said holding out her hand for a shake.

"Damolà" I said taking her hand and immediately her eyes widened in surprise and recognition.

She remembered me.

Adedoyin Ayeni

CHAPTER THREE

DARÀSIMI

"Damolà" I heard him say my hands still in his as I immediately recognized his facial features in an instant.

It was him. My first love who stood right in front of me with my hands in his. I couldn't tell if he remembered who I was but I did and I didn't know how to feel about it.

I slowly removed my hands from his as the tension between us started to get thick as I stared off into the view. He's changed so much. He grew up to be anything as I imagined. Tall, muscular, talented and extremely good looking. His facial features and smooth brown skin completely knocking me off my feet.

Oh my gosh! Am I dreaming? Is this one of those wet dreams? Or is this real!

"I also can't stop being marveled by the view it's amazing." he said his deep voice sounding like music to me with his thick New York accent.

Turning to look at him only to find him already staring intently at me. I immediately turned my eyes away from his wondering if he could already tell who I was.

"Why do you keep turning away from me?" He asked in an observant tone.

"Nothing. I'm just tired" I lied

"Do you live in the school dorms?" He asked curiously.

"Yes."

"Can I have your phone number?" "Why?"

"Because I want to see you again." he answered staring deeply into my eyes causing my heart to beat really fast.

"I don't know if I want to though" I muttered

"I doubt you're telling the truth simì." He answered stretching out his hand waiting for my phone.

Taking in a deep breath I brought it out and gave it to him as I watched him input his number and save it before sending himself a text on WhatsApp before finally giving it back to me.

"I'll be in touch. It was nice seeing you again simì" he said with a smirk before walking away and that's when it hit me.

He remembered who I was.

Lia walked towards me holding a can of beer as her eyes followed Damolà's leaving presence with curiosity in them.

"You know the really hot singer?" She asked

"Something like that." I muttered slightly my heart still beating as I remembered the way his eyes stared intently at mine.

"He's really good looking. Do you think he's dating anyone?" she said absentmindedly as she gazed at the entrance.

Not knowing how to reply to her question I kept quiet instead my mind replaying what just happened between us. She noticed how quiet I was deciding to break the silence as she immediately hooked her arm in mine with a playful smile on her face.

"So simì, are you having fun?"

"Yeah I am, thanks for bringing me out here tonight" I replied pushing all thoughts about Damolà to the very back of my mind.

"You're welcome. c'mon I want to introduce you to my friends" she dragged me off to a far corner at the rooftop bar.

A group of four people all sat around a small table chatting happily and drinking. Their voices went slightly quiet at our presence with their curious eyes staring at me wondering who I was. Immediately my social anxiety kicked in and I felt really shy to look at them.

"Guys this is my roommate simì.." Lia introduced happily

"Hi." I squeaked

"Hey I'm Dax" a really tall and lean white guy with short brown hair stood up as he introduced himself with a smile which relaxed my nerves a bit.

"Hello." I said shyly

Lia immediately found a seat for the both of us as we sat down the eyes of her friends still on me.

"That's Pearl, Priya and Bella" she introduced the others who sat around the table with us.

Pearl was light skinned with short and thick Afro hair just like mine and she had it in two puffy buns on her head. She looked really sweet and calm with the way she sat. I felt like pearl had a gentle personality. Priya was Indian with really smooth brown skin and long black hair. She looked exotic and her ears and nose were pierced with gold trinkets and her hands were decorated with henna. Bella was white with ginger red hair and hazel eyes. She looked intense with how hard her eyes wouldn't stop accessing me but I didn't let it get to me.

"Hey welcome to NYU. Lia already told us about you. It's nice to meet you" Priya said with a soft smile.

"Thanks. it's really nice to meet you guys"

"When Lia mentioned you she didn't do justice enough and talk about how beautiful you are" Dax complimented making me blush slightly.

"Wow thank you."

Bella just groaned in annoyance giving him a sharp

look " Relax your balls Dax, stop hitting on her. She just got here for Christ's sake"

I just watched Dax smirk in mischief at that giving her an amused look.

Was something going on between them?

"Don't mind Dax simì he's just a huge playboy and can't keep it in his pants" Lia blurted out crudely making me giggle in amusement.

"Hey mind you know I wasn't expecting her to look so ravishing okay. And you know I always compliment a beauty when I see one" Dax replied defensively making me smile harder.

"It's fine Lia and thank you Dax." I said making him wink at me.

At the corner of my eyes i noticed how Bella's features didn't seem relaxed or happy about how Dax seemed to like me.

Okay. it's very obvious she likes him. I should be careful.

"So simì what's your major? Are you an undergrad?" Pearl asked, her voice really small confirming my suspicions about her gentle character.

"No i'm a masters student. Food Engineering"

"Wow! Beautiful and intelligent. Double threat!" Dax exclaimed in admiration making me blush shyly.

He was really cute and so playful.

"Dax will you chill the fuck out your testosterone levels are like so high right now." Priya scolded playfully making all of us laugh except Bella who just scrolled through her phone.

"Yeah guys my roommate is an engineer. I feel so proud and entitled already. How many of you know engineers. Uhh?" Lia boasted playfully making me laugh softly.

"Oh shut up Lia." Bella added making everyone laugh.

"Pearl is an undergrad studying literature, Priya is a law student, Bella is a grad student trying to get her masters in fashion designing while Dax is an undergrad studying veterinary medicine" Lia explained making me look at all of them in admiration.

They were all really impressive.

"So where are you from simì?" Bella asked surprised that she was actually talking to me.

"Oh i just arrived from Nigeria." I answered.

They looked at me curiously probably not knowing where exactly my country was located. I smiled softly at that not exactly blaming them.

"It's in Africa"

Their eyes immediately twinkled in recognition as they all mumbled finally understanding where I was from.

"Wow you flew all the way from Africa? That's so cool" Priya chirped in making smile.

"Yeah. Thanks"

"Do you have a boyfriend simì?" Dax asked straightforwardly surprising me and causing Lia to hit him on the head.

"What?" He asked confused raising both his shoulders.

I realized that they all stared at me waiting for an answer. "I'm single."

"Really?" Dax asked his voice sounding excited causing me to let out a chuckle.

"Aww simì I'm sure you'll find someone.New York

City is big place. Maybe your soul mate is here waiting" Priya added making me nod my head.

"Maybe."

"I'm single too" Dax inputed almost immediately making me let out a laugh.

He was trying so hard it was really cute.

"Dude give it a rest" Lia groaned in slight annoyance.

He just picked up his beer giving me a small wink with a mischievous smile on his lips. The night went by pretty fast and I was starting to have fun with Lia's friends. They weren't bad and they made me feel really comfortable as I got to know them better. Dax asked me out sort of to take me on a tour around New York and I turned down the offer politely saying how I haven't fully settled in yet.

But I knew he wasn't giving up that easily.

Sadly I had to leave first and go back to my dorm because I was becoming really tired. I had to go into the school's campus tomorrow to sort out all of my applications and get my schedule for my classes so I needed to rest. They all understood and promised to keep in touch. Dax booked me an Uber to take me back and I was really grateful for his help since I just got here and didn't really know my way around. Once the Uber showed up I hugged each of them before leaving finally.

♪♪♪♪♪

The sun shone really brightly as I stood right outside of the Admission's office. I had just finished everything that had to do with my registration. My class schedule was already sent to my email as I stared at it on my phone. I had just five courses and one technical course which were arranged properly at days during the week. I wasn't fully starting classes until next week and I considered taking Dax on that offer of touring around New York with him but I felt a bit stupid going back on my word so I just decided to go back to my dorm and sleep until Lia gets back and we can probably go out together.

My phone rang almost immediately as I brought it out from my purse the screen turned on to show Damolà's name. My heart beat increased by a millisecond as I wondered whether to pick it up or not. Staring at my phone I decided to answer it curious to hear what he had to say.

"Hello"

"Hi simì" his deep voice called making my stomach do little flips. "How're you?" I asked softly

"I'm fine. Are you free?" He asked making my breath quicken slightly in anticipation.

"Maybe."

"Have lunch with me"

"You're not even going to ask if I want to?" I threw in slight annoyance at his unnerving confidence.

"You know I don't like to go around the bush simi" he said his voice dangerously low making me gulp.

I took in a deep breath deciding to just play his game.

"I don't know my way around New York" I answered honestly.

"I'll pick you up. Where are you?" He pushed on.

"I'm currently in school standing right outside of the Admission's building." I answered.

"Okay, wait for me. I'll be right there" and with that he hung up making me stare at my phone in slight shock.

Bringing out a small mirror from my purse i checked my appearance and face hoping I looked good enough. I didn't want to look tired while having lunch with my first love. My outfit was okay, I was putting on a white summer backless dress with puffy sleeves and shiny black flats and my hair was styled in the usual puffy ponytail. Putting up some final touches to my face with a little bit of brown powder and applying my strawberry lip gloss. I smiled at myself in the small mirror satisfied with how I looked.

Just as I finished a Black Bronco pulled up right in front of me surprising me at how shiny it looked. The door opened and he stepped out looking like a male model.

He was wearing blue jeans and a white short sleeved shirt which looked really snug on him and on his feet were air Jordan's. He was glowing quite literally and wore pair of gold circular rimmed glasses on his face making him look like a hot nerd.

Oh my days!

His eyes met mine and i melted at the intensity of his gaze. He was the most beautiful man i had ever laid eyes on and I don't think he saw himself like that because it was obvious he was a very simple person but then the simplicity in how he looked made him look so much better. I watched his eyes rake every inch of my body before landing back on my eyes.

"Let's go" he said simply making me roll my eyes at

his rudeness before walking towards him and stepping into his car with no words said.

He entered back into the car starting it and driving us to someplace that god knows where.

CHAPTER FOUR

DAMOLÀ

We both sat opposite each other at the fine restaurant I brought us to. I couldn't stop myself from staring at her, she was beautiful. Beautiful in such a way that made me want to touch her, to kiss her, to hold her and to make her mine. I could tell she wasn't fully comfortable around me yet and I planned on changing that really soon. Her eyes finally stopped looking around the restaurant and returned to mine only to find me staring at her the intensity making her jump slightly making me smirk. At least I had an effect on her.

Taking a sip of my coffee and deciding to stop staring

at her as I watched her from the corner of my eye fidget with her fingers.

"How did you get home last night?" I asked curiously bringing her out from her thoughts as I tried to get her to relax around me.

"I took an Uber" she replied causing me to nod at that.

"Why did you want to have lunch with me?" She asked seeming a bit confused.

"Because I wanted to see you.."

"It was a long time ago Damolà there's really no need to try." she cut in almost immediately and that's when I saw the look in her eyes.

She still had feelings for me.

"More reason we have to catch up." I disagreed with her giving her a challenging look.

One thing she knew about me was how stubborn I was and I could tell she knew I wasn't going to back down anytime soon.

She took in a deep breath to calm her nerves as I watched her pick up her cup of latte before locking eyes with mine the intensity making me weak in the knees.

"Okay, let's catch up. You're in New York, I'm in New York. A very big coincidence."

"Yeah it really is especially when I never thought I'd get to see you again" I said with a slight chuckle my words getting her attention.

"Your mum told us you guys were moving to UK"

"We didn't move to the UK we came back to New York" I answered her.

"You didn't say good bye before you left." She muttered softly the emotions in her eyes difficult for her to hide.

"I couldn't." I said quietly as I cleared my throat unable to currently look her in her the eye.

"It's fine. I'm just.. i'm glad you're okay. You seem to be doing fine. I just never imagined you'd be a musician"

"It just happened. One day I was at my worst and I didn't know how exactly I could express my pain and found myself writing and once I was done and I looked at it I realized that they were lyrics." I explained as I remembered my words surprising her.

"Wow."

"Yeah."

"How about you? How're your mum and sisters?" I asked softly as I watched her relax more in her seat.

"They're doing fine. I honestly miss them" she chuckled with a small smile on her face making her look so beautiful.

"You'll be fine. How're you finding New York?" I asked curiously.

"Not going to lie but it's really busy, my god I've only been here for like a day and it's so hectic every-where" she said sounding stressed in a cute way making me snort at that.

"You'll get used to it don't worry."

"I hope so but it's a nice city. I mean I've always dreamt about coming here and now that I'm here it still feels like a dream" she said with a soft smile on her face making me smile too.

"I'm proud of you simì . And the fact that you grew up so well is amazing" I complimented with a smile making her blush in surprise.

"Thanks Damì"

"Have you made any friends yet?" I asked curiously.

"Just a few, I'm not really much of a social person so

I doubt I'll be out and about in the city" she confessed honestly.

"It's the same for me. I spend most of my nights either at work or in my house drinking wine and catching up on my favorite episodes of CSI" I confessed honestly making her laugh quite a bit.

"Really? Didn't peg you as the anti-social type" she said criticizing me.

"Why do you say so?" I asked curiously

"Well that's because back in Nigeria it was so easy for you to make friends. You were quite popular back then" she answered giving me a look.

"I think it was because I was the kid that just came back from America and i had an accent because i only enjoyed playing with you" I said in all honesty making her smile in amusement.

"Really? Well right now I'm honored but back then I honestly wanted you off my back. You were so annoying and never left me alone" she groaned playfully making me laugh softly.

"You were really fun to be around and I loved bugging you."

"I know. I still remember the time you told everyone that we were married. Ugh! Like no boy would approach me and girls didn't want to be friends with me because apparently Dami was my husband" she said shaking her head at my antics.

I admit I was quite mischievous while I was a kid but I only did all that because I had a huge crush on her and I was jealous whenever I saw her talk to other boys.

"I honestly miss those times. I had fun and that was really the only time I remember myself being truly happy." I said noticing how her facial features changed softly trying to understand my words.

"How come? What happened after you left?" She asked looking concerned

"My mum fell really sick. She had breast cancer" I answered as I watched her eyes widen in shock

"Did she make it?".

"No. I lost her when I was fifteen" I heard her gasp in surprise at that as I looked at her eyes to see the emotion it held.

"Oh I'm so sorry Damolà, I'm really sorry. I know how much you loved her." she consoled trying her best not to shed a tear

"It's fine, I'm also really sorry about your dad. I never planned to just leave like that. Things were just really out of my control" I apologized as I noticed how her face fell at the mention of her father.

I remembered how broken she was when her dad fell sick. He was diagnosed with a neck tumor and just when we all thought he was getting better he died and that was the last time we ever saw him. He was everything to her and also a mentor to me. I never got to know my dad, but I knew hers and he was just like a father to me too. And just when she really needed me by her side i was on a plane going back to New York without saying goodbye.

"It's fine dami." She said and I noticed how she no longer wanted to talk about her father and I wondered why.

"I missed you simi" I confessed as I watched her eyes snap back to mine in surprise. We held each other's gaze as I waited for her to say something but she just kept quiet and I took in a deep breath deciding to break the silence.

"I'm a Doctor specializing in surgical oncology" I blurted out deciding to stop hiding it.

"Really?" She asked in shock

"Yes."

"What about music?"

"It's my passion too. Your dad was my inspiration simi. Remember how he used to teach us both how to play the guitar?" I said trying to bring in the nostalgia but I noticed her facial features harden.

"Dami, please." she muttered softly sounding really broken.

She didn't want to talk about him.

"I should drop you off, c'mon. My lunch break is almost over" I said as I got up from my seat with her looking up to me.

She stood up too piking up her purse our eyes still locked on each other.

"I missed you too dami" I heard her say before I watched her walk out the door with me on her tail a small smile on my face.

She missed me.

♩♪♩♪♪

Seated in my office as I read through some medical journals my door opened and my female best friend walked in with a smile on her face as she held a small piece of cake in her hands. I removed my reading glasses from my eyes as I watched her take a seat in front of me her eyes twinkling in amusement as I smiled at her. Laura and I met while we were both in med school. She was the only girl I allowed get close to me and could tolerate because she understood my need for personal boundaries, was extremely intelligent and we had a lot of things in common.

For example we both hated socializing and people and took pride in our accomplishments.

She was also an oncologist but her specialty was brain tumor. She was really good at her job and I respected her a lot.

"Guess who just tried to hit on me at the cafeteria?" She said trying to hold back a snort. "Don't tell me it was Dr Frazier again." I answered with a shake of my head.

"Today's his birthday and gave me a piece of his cake so I decided to share it with you" she said with a smile as I watched her take a small piece of it.

Laura was among the top doctors in Williams's Cancer Research Institute and also she was beautiful. Tall, slim, smooth white skin with nice facial features so she was in serious high demand among the single male doctors but she refused to date anyone which confused me a lot. Her last relationship was during our fellowship as interns and it didn't really last quite long. Whenever I brought it up and asked why she refuses to date anyone she just says none of the men she's met do it for her and I honestly wonder what it meant but I decided to just not bother anymore.

I mean it's her life

"It's fine, I'm not really hungry for cake"

She just shrugged as she continued to eat it. "By the way where were you? I came to look for you to eat lunch with me and your head nurse told me you stepped out for lunch"

"Yeah I had to meet someone" I answered

"Who?" She asked curiously

"A close friend from home."

"Really? Oh okay. so did you guys catch up?"

"Yeah it was alright. Planning on having lunch with her again tomorrow."

"Her? She's a girl?" She asked in surprise

"Yeah."

"Can I join you guys tomorrow? Please. I really don't want to sit all alone again at the cafeteria, Frazier would want to use it to his advantage. Please Dami" She begged with a pout making me roll my eyes playfully.

"Okay, fine. You can join us tomorrow"

"Yes! Really can't wait to see who she is" she added making me stare at her in slight confusion.

"I'm just curious. You don't exactly have any close friends apart from Tom and I, plus you've never mentioned her before so I just wanna see how it came about. Besides a friend of yours is a friend of mine" she said with a smile making me chuckle.

"Alright, I've heard you. Now please leave so I can catch up on what I'm reading"

"Rude much?" She glared playfully making me shake my head in amusement. "Bye Laura"

She just stuck her tongue out at me playfully before finally leaving me alone to my book as she left my office.

CHAPTER FIVE

Daràsimi

My phone rang waking me up from my sleep. The sky was still dark and across my room I could still see Lia asleep underneath her covers. I wondered who it was that was calling me this late when the screen flashed to see that I was getting a video call from my two closest friends back in Nigeria. Answering the call and connecting to my Air Pods so I wouldn't disturb Lia while on the phone with them.

"Daraaaa! What did you mean by the text that you sent?" My bestie Sharon screamed over the phone her face showing up on the screen with her boyfriend Ola next to her.

"Guys do you realize what the time is over here?" I sleepily groaned rubbing my eyes as I switched on my bedside lamp illuminating my face so they could see me clearly on the screen.

"I told her that it'll be very late over there due to the time difference and you'd probably be sleeping but trust Sharon to never listen to me" Ola said apologetically giving me a soft look making me roll my eyes at my besties antics.

"Sharon why don't you ever listen to your boyfriend, can't we not just discuss this when it's bright and sunny" I groaned tiredly

"As if I know when it's bright in New York"

"You have your phone sharon and you can check the world clock" I argued trying to let her let me sleep.

"Another time, now tell me. Did you really meet Damolà??" She asked very curiously.

I took in a deep breath realizing that she wasn't releasing me from this conversation anytime soon. I sat up on my bed holding my phone up, my face coming up fully on screen.

"Yeah I did. At a party on my first night here"

"Oh my gosh! How? What're the odds?? I mean it's been so long, you never thought you'd ever get to see him again" she exclaimed in shock.

"I know right. It was totally crazy babes. Especially when he totally recognized me at first glance. It was when he told me his name did I fully recognize him. I was shocked babe"

"Wow, oh my gosh. So what now? Did you meet him after that night?"

"Yeah, he called me yesterday and asked me to lunch. I was so shocked when I got his call honestly." I explained still in awe of everything.

"Aww.Wow babe I'm so happy for you though, I mean all of your relationships have been shitty. Maybe this is finally your silver lining" she said sounding hopeful making me give her a look.

"Don't make this weird babe, nothing's going to happen between us. He probably might be dating someone *sef*. It was just a weird coincidence that we met each other again. I doubt he even likes me like that" I said completely putting the idea off.

"How do you know? Babe the fact that you guys met again after so many years is just fate and destiny trying to bring you two together. You said he was your first love, you guys kissed. He might still have feelings for you" she pushed trying to get me to see her point.

"We were still kids, and the kiss was a mistake. We both didn't know what we were doing."

"Ugh! Dara why don't you always see the positive side in everything. You need this. You need to be loved for once babe, I want you happy and I know Damolà's the one for you"

"You've never even met him Babe" I said giving her another weird look causing her to groan in annoyance.

"Yeah but you talked my ears off about him for so long. I didn't need to meet him to already see that the two of had something special that sadly ended before it could even start" she argued blindly.

"Ola has she been watching those tarot reading videos on TikTok lately because she's acting really delusional" I asked calling his attention.

He just smiled and shrugged, he knows better than to come in when his girlfriend was trying to play Cupid for me. He's learnt his lesson once.

"You're just over analyzing everything Sharon, I doubt he still remembers anything we did back then. Besides he's changed"

"How do you mean?"

"I mean he's not the same like he used to be. He seems cold and distant and talks a bit rude." I said with a thought as I remembered our conversations.

"You can change him"

"Ugh Sharon, can't you see the context of what I'm saying??"

"Babe you don't know what he's been through in those years that changed him. The same way you've changed is the same way he's changed too. You both grew up. Please make this work dara" she pleaded with me with a warm look in her eyes.

I sighed deeply deciding to just agree with her to pacify her " Alright Babe, I'll try."

"Good girl." She said with a smile giving me a thumbs up.

"Now that everything's settled, can you please release me so I can sleep" I begged her as she released a soft laugh.

"Okay, go to sleep. Let's talk when it's brighter" "Thank you" I said finally.

"Alright babe, love you"

"Love you too, bye Ola" and with that I hung up and went back to sleep pushing everything she said about dami and I to the very back of my mind.

♪♪♫♪♪

Standing right outside of a cosmetics pop up store with a small bag filled with new cosmetics and skincare products i just got for myself my phone immediately started to ring with the screen flashing and Damolà's name showing on it. My eyes scrunched up in slight confusion wondering why he was calling me this afternoon deciding to pick it up and hear what he had to say.

"Hello"

"Hi simì, are you on school campus?" He asked forwardly.

"No I'm not, Why?" I asked

"Wanted us to have lunch together." He stated simply.

"Oh at where exactly? I could come meet you there" I offered politely.

"I'll send you the address, take a taxi." He ordered.

"Oh okay" and with that he hung up.

Getting down from the taxi with the bag filled with the stuff I just bought I stood right outside of the restaurant. Walking in I sighted him sitting down at a nice corner of the restaurant and he didn't seem to be alone. Taking small strides towards where he sat I finally stood right in front of the both of them. His eyes finally noticing my presence he gave a curt nod gesturing for me to take my seat at the opposite side of the booth.

My eyes finally noticed who sat next to him and it was a girl, a really pretty white girl. She offered me a smile and I wondered who she was and why she was with him not really returning back the smile since I was confused about what was actually going on.

"Hey" I greeted finally breaking the silence.

"Hey, what's that in your hands?"he asked curiously gesturing to the plastic bag I currently held.

"Just some new cosmetics and skincare products I might need" I answered.

"Hi I'm Laura" the girl introduced with an outstretched hand beaming happily.

"Hi i'm simi" I replied taking her hand before shortly releasing it.

"I know and it's really nice to meet you. Hope you

don't mind me cutting in on you guys lunch?" She asked batting her eyelashes in a really cringe way that made her seem innocent.

Was she his girlfriend? Is he about to introduce me to his woman or something, was that why he called me?

"It's fine, I'd have just liked it if dami told me that he would be bringing along his girlfriend so I wouldn't be so surprised to meet you"

"Laura isn't my girlfriend simì" he immediately said with a curt look on his face.

Oh.

Laura looked at the both of us seeming to sense the tension before breaking the weird silence with a really high pitched laugh confusing me as I wondered what was so funny.

"Oh silly, Damolà and I aren't dating. He's my best friend" she said with an amused smile on her face.

The word best friend hit me and I raised my eyes to meet his in question. I never thought that he had a girl best friend and even if he did shouldn't he have checked with me first before inviting her on our lunch.

I mean the audacity!

"I just really didn't want to eat alone at the cafeteria today because I'm currently trying to avoid someone so I begged him to bring me along. I hope it's not too much of a bother, I'd hate that I ruined your lunch date" she apologized with a soft look on her face.

Waiting for him to disagree with her that this wasn't a lunch date but he said nothing and I just bit my lower lip in slight annoyance.

"It's fine Laura, I really don't mind and it's nice to meet you" I finally replied ignoring Dami's intense stares.

"Okay. We work together. I've honestly known this grumpy bear since med school" she said with a baby voice squeezing both his cheeks as I watched him playfully shrug her off him.

Uhm what exactly is happening right now??

"Oh I see, that's really nice"

"What about you? Not going to lie but Dami never mentioned you. I honestly didn't know he had another close friend apart from his best friend tom and I. So don't blame me for wanting to be so curious and excited to meet you because this guy rarely keeps friends" she explained giving me a complete once over with her eyes starting to make me a bit uncomfortable.

"We just recently met again after a long time .We didn't really keep in touch all those years."

"That explains why I'm just getting to know who you are" she nodded in understanding.

"Can you please excuse me" I said taking fast strides to the ladies room needing some air. I was starting to get really suffocated in there.

Once I was in the restroom after looking around and finding out it was empty. I took in a huge breath my heart beating really fast. Throughout the period Laura kept on talking I could feel

Dami's calculating eyes on me. He wasn't saying anything but he was watching my every movement and that got my skin to prickle a bit causing goosebumps to erupt. Not long after I entered Dami walked in locking the door behind him leaving the both of us all alone in the restroom and my body immediately went on over-drive with my blood pumping really fast.

He took slow strides towards me and i could see him clearly this time. The air between us was really thick as his eyes never left mine for once. He looked really good in black suit pants and a coral blue shirt and black leather loafers.

"Why did you leave like that?" He asked softly his deep voice causing my tummy to do tiny flips.

"I needed to breathe and your best friend was talking my ear off" I said quite rudely causing him to smirk at that.

"She was just trying to be nice"

"Really? Why didn't you tell me that she was going to be here?" I asked giving him a hard look not letting his build intimidate me.

"Because I didn't think you'd mind" he said and this time he stood right in front of me and i could inhale his sweet manly scent.

He smelled like expensive cologne.

"Well I very much mind Damolà, I don't like being forced or bombarded into situations that wasn't planned" I threw back in annoyance.

He walked closer causing me to walk backwards unable to stand still with him being this close to me. He raised a challenging eyebrow to that moving closer trying to close the gap between us but i still moved backwards. A small smirk grew at the sides of his lips before i felt his hands grip both my arms and push me to the wall cornering me and forcing me to look up into his eyes.

Suddenly the air between us grew really thick and I couldn't utter a word as i stared into his eyes feeling struck.

"Are you jealous princess?" He whispered softly causing the hairs on my neck to stand straight at the pet name he called me.

Only my dad called me that and he knew it.

I glared heavily at him hating the fact that he called me that watching how that seem to amuse him more.

"You're jealous aren't you princess." He repeated wanting to push me to my limits.

"Don't call me that." I warned

"But why? You're my sweet little princess and right now I can smell the jealousy off you" he pushed on his fingers softly playing with my hair.

"I hate you!" I shouted in anger which just made him chuckle deeply.

"Do you really princess?" he asked with a small smile causing my stomach to the little jump flips at that. His eyes slowly wandered down to my lips and I waited in anticipation about what he wanted to do.

He leaned in an inch away from my face our eyes

heavily locked on each other. My breath coming out in slow pants and the slow anticipation killing me softly. Closing my eyes thinking he was about to kiss me he raised his face away from mine as I internally groaned at that.

"I won't bring her along to anymore of our lunch dates." I heard him whisper in my ears causing my eyes to jerk open in surprise at that.

I looked back at his eyes as I watched his lip quirk up in a small smile before he released me from his hold and finally walking out of the rest room leaving me to my thoughts and already messed up emotions.

CHAPTER SIX

DAMOLÀ

Sitting back down on the chair unable to wipe off the small smile that was starting to grow on my face as I thought about how much of an effect I had on her. She was jealous from the minute she walked into the restaurant and saw me sitting with another woman it annoyed her and I liked it so much. I already knew that she didn't like being bombarded into situations because she hadn't changed much.

"Is your friend okay?" Laura asked her voice filled with slight confusion getting my attention.

"Yeah she's fine, I'm sure she'll be right out soon" I

said with a smirk on my lips really enjoying the current situation.

Not soon after simì appeared her facial expression calm but I knew it was all a facade. I could see right through her and she knew it which bothered her more. She took steady steps walking back into her seat refusing to look me in the eyes which just made my smirk widen in excitement. She was just too cute.

"I'm sorry I left like that Laura, I wasn't really feeling too well" she apologized kindly. Laura just returned her apology with a smile.

"Simì what do you have planned this weekend?" I asked purposefully trying to turn her attention to me.

She just looked up at me with those beautiful eyes trying to hide how much I had an effect on her. I watched her give me a fake smile making my smirk widen in mischief as I dared her with my eyes to ignore me.

"Nothing, why?" She asked, her tone sounding slightly annoyed at that.

"I have a show I'm performing at on Saturday night and I want you to come"

My invite seemed to surprise her and I figured she wasn't expecting me ask her that.

"Oh, okay. where is it?" She asked sounding really interested.

"It's at a jazz club, they needed someone to open the show and I was invited" I answered

"Really? Wow, that's very impressive"

"Thanks, I'll send you the address of the place"

"Alright then." She replied with a genuine smile on her face causing me to smile softly at that.

"So what're you doing in New York simì?" Laura asked all of a sudden getting all of our attentions.

"I got a scholarship for my masters to study Food Engineering in NYU" she replied her words slightly surprising Laura.

"Really? Oh wow. That's impressive"

"Thanks"

"So you and Dami are like childhood friends?"

"Yeah we grew up together while he was in Nigeria and lost contact after he left" she answered as she slowly ate her food.

"Really? For how long?" Laura asked seeming really interested in our story.

"He left when I was eleven and I'm currently twenty-one so it's been ten years since we last saw each other" she replied as I watched Laura's mouth open wide in shock at that.

I can't believe it's been ten years, god I missed her so much.

Raising my eyes to meet hers we locked gazes and I could tell she was surprised too at how long we've been apart and I wanted so badly to make up for lost time. She was it for me and no one else. If only there was some way for me to show her. To get her to be mine, forever.

"And you guys met how?" Laura asked pressing on.

Simì chuckled softly before answering her "We met at a rooftop bar just some days ago by coincidence. I never imagined he'd be in New York or that he was a musician. It all happened so fast"

"It was the same for me too, imagine how surprised I was to see you standing right in front of me as I performed. For a while I thought it was a dream" I muttered with a deep chuckle making her let out a soft laugh.

We might've been apart for ten years butt right now watching her seated across from me smiling happily those years mean nothing. This current chapter that just started between us were the ones that meant everything to me.

"Wow fate really decided to bring you two together. That's crazy. Feels like a scene out of a movie but then it's real and it's like wow" Laura said still feeling awestruck.

"I guess if you put it like that it seems fate worked in our favors but I honestly think it was just coincidence" she said simply making me slightly annoyed at how she wasn't seeing the significance of us meeting each other again.

"It wasn't coincidence simì, it was fate." I spoke out getting both their attentions as I corrected her. I knew that she was trying to fight her feelings, to deny the fact that she feels connected to me so she's trying to make it seem like nothing.

She's lying to herself and denying that what we have isn't real. But it was real and deep down it scared her. I could see it.

She gave me a look hating the fact that I called her out on what she said as I watched her pick up a glass of water in annoyance and drinking it before answering me.

"What makes you think it was fate Damolà?"

"Because I thought about you every freaking day of

my life hoping that one day I'll finally get to see you again." I confessed bluntly my words hitting her as I watched her beautiful eyes widen in surprise.

"Wow dami. That was uh." Laura said in slight shock unable to get over what I just said sensing the current tension in the air.

"I should go. Laura it was really nice to meet you." she said in a rush picking up her things about to leave making me scoff in disbelief.

I can't believe she's trying to run away. Really?!

"Oh. okay." I heard Laura say before I watched simì walk out the restaurant without saying anything to me.

I could have followed her out and stopped her as I tried to get her understand but I'll let her have this one. You can keep on running princess, I won't stop chasing until I finally have you and when that happens I'm never letting you go.

♪♪♪♪♪♪

The car ride back to the hospital was oddly quiet, Laura wasn't talking much or asking questions which I thought was weird because she's not the type to ever keep quiet.

I guess she wasn't expecting what happened at lunch and still trying to process it.

"Your silence is oddly pleasing" I said as I watched her turn to give me a glare causing me to laugh softly.

"Who's that girl to you Dami? I mean you've never ever mentioned knowing anyone from Nigeria or having family back home. The only family we all know is your mum and now I'm hearing this and I just don't know what to think" she said turning to give me a questioning look.

I don't blame her for wanting to understand what was going on. She might be my best friend but my personal boundaries never let me open up my past to her. Tom is only an exception because he was close enough to be a brother to me and that was only because he's seen me through my worst times.

"That girl is my first love Laura. I never told you about her because she was from my past and my personal boundaries didn't allow me talk to you about it." I explained as I heard her sigh loudly to that.

"So she's the girl that's been in your heart for so long. That has refused you from ever letting people in" she repeated turning to look at me with an emotion I've never seen her show before in her eyes.

"Simì isn't the reason why I put up walls but yeah she's the girl that I've not been able to move on from." I answered still trying to figure out why Laura was acting a bit strange.

This side of her was new and I didn't know how to walk around it.

"Why didn't you ever look for her?" She asked curiously.

"Things weren't the best at that time, I was trying to survive. It didn't seem like the right thing to do at that time especially after I left without even telling her goodbye." I answered.

"Do you still like her?" She asked softly waiting for my answer as I stopped the car finally in front of the hospital turning it off.

"Yes i still like her Laura" I answered turning to look at her only to see her eyes softly watering as she took in a deep breath as I wondered what exactly was wrong.

Why's she acting strange.

"Wow that's surprising but okay."

"Laura are you okay? You're acting really strange." I asked starting to feel really worried.

She just gave a light humorless laugh as i watched her clean the tears threatening to fall in her eyes with her fingers before answering me.

"Yeah I'm fine, it's just allergies"

"Oh okay" I answered not knowing what to do or say completely new to this side of her.

"I don't think she still likes you dami" she said after finally calming herself down.

"What makes you say that?" I asked with a raised eyebrow.

"Because she ran away right after you confessed your feelings to her. If you want my advice, I'd say you should move on. There are a lot more fishes in the sea" she said giving me a really intense look her words annoying me.

"Let's talk later okay, think about it grumpy bear" she said with a playful smile as she squeezed the side of my cheeks before finally getting down from my car.

I just sat in my car unable to move, Laura's words deeply sinking in as I thought about what she said. Picking up my phone and dialing simi's number. It rang for a while before she finally picked up her sweet voice filling up my ears.

"Hey princess"

"It's simì, stop calling me that!" She snapped in annoyance causing me to chuckle at that.

"Why did you leave like that, are you trying to run away from me?" I asked with a slight smirk on my lips.

"Yes." She said simply her reply surprising me. I recollected myself immediately from the surprise of her honesty before saying anything.

"Why princess?"

"Because you're being how you used to be when we were kids, you won't lay off my back. You keep on pushing and following me everywhere" she answered sounding really frustrated.

"And it bothers you?" "Very much yes!" "Why simì?"

"I don't know.. but stop. Stop doing any of this, stop pushing,"

"Stop fighting simì, I'm not going to stop. I'm never ever going to stop. I lost you once and I'm not about to do it again. Not when fate decided to play nice this time" I answered firmly her breathing sounding uneven over the phone.

"We were kids Damolà, we didn't know what we were doing." She pleaded trying to get me to understand and stop trying.

"I always knew what I was doing simì and deep down you know I'm right"

She just gave a scoff to that as I heard her laugh humorlessly "you're acting delusional dami"

"Am I princess? Because last i remembered you wanted me to kiss you so badly in that restroom. I wonder who's really the delusional one here?" I deadpanned as the line went quiet, my lips lifting up in a smirk realizing I just caught her in her game.

"You're wrong" she whispered

I just laughed at her weak way of letting me know that I've finally caught her.

"You know what princess, you're right, we were kids back then but now I'm a grown man and you're a grown woman so this time I'm going to do it the grown up way."

"Damì, please." she said sounding really vulnerable.

"Let's talk later simì, you think about everything i just said and what you really want" and with that I hung up leaving her to messy emotions as i buried my head on the steering wheel wondering how I was going to get myself out of this mess.

CHAPTER SEVEN

DARÀSIMI

TWELVE YEARS AGO

"Simì! Simì!" My mum shouted my name from the veranda her voice sounding really annoyed as I ran back into the compound trying my very best not to get caught by her. I wasn't supposed to be outside but I sneaked out to go and collect some set of story books from my classmates.

I wasn't properly looking at where I was going heading smack down with something or someone actually as we both hit the floor with me lying right on top of him with my storybooks scattered all over the ground.

Raising my head slightly and mumbling from the pain from falling. I looked down only to be met with the softest black pupils I'd ever seen staring right at me in surprise none of us moving from the spot on the ground.

My mum's voice got louder and closer and i shivered in fear not wanting her to catch me. The boy I still laid on top off gave me an incredulous look trying to push me off him but I just stayed still shaking my head profusely and trying to get him to keep quiet so my mum wouldn't find me but he wouldn't stop resisting. He was cute that's for sure but if I didn't keep him quiet as soon as possible he was going to get me in serious trouble and I couldn't afford for it to happen.

"Get off me!" He shouted rudely making my eyes widen in annoyance and immediately giving him a pleading look to shut up but he still wasn't getting it and my mum was getting really close to where we both laid.

"Please stop talking" I begged.

"No get off me" he ordered rudely his way of speaking sounding really different to me. He had an American accent.

"I can't, I'm hiding from my mum" I whispered

"That's your problem, not mine. So get off!" He

snapped rudely, getting on my last nerve. He was talking too much and I needed to shut him up.

Not waiting for him to say anything more I kissed him. My lips colliding with his soft ones immediately shutting him up. His eyes opened in shock while mine was shut deeply unable to look him in the eye while I kissed him. My mum's voice finally reduced and almost immediately he pushed me off him with so much force causing me to land on my butt as he stared at me in shock wondering what I just did to him.

Not waiting to hear what he had to say I picked up all of my story books and immediately ran away from the scene hoping to never run into him again as I realized that I just gave him my first kiss.

♪♪♪♪♪♪

I sat outside in our veranda reading some of the story-books I collected from my classmates when my mind immediately went to the kiss. Groaning in annoyance and slight disgust I hit my head wondering why I did some-thing as crazy as that. I can't believe I kissed a strange boy just so my mum wouldn't catch me. As I read my books, I felt the presence of someone. Raising my head from my book only to be met with the boy I kissed some minutes ago staring straight at me with a mischievous smile playing on his lips completely shocking me as I stared up at him with my mouth wide open.

"Simì I see you've met our new neighbor" my dad said coming out to meet us right in the veranda with a smile on his face.

"Neighbor?" I questioned in surprise still staring at him before turning to look at my dad.

"Yes princess, He and his mum just moved down from America. They rented out the flat on the ground floor" my dad explained still smiling happily as he placed his hand on the boy's shoulder.

"Damolà this is my eldest daughter, Simì"

The boy just grinned playfully his smile making me feel weird in my tummy before I heard him say.

"Hi simì, it's really nice to meet you"

My dad just smiled not realizing what was currently happening before walking out of the veranda leaving the both of us alone. I just faced down to my books refusing to look him in the eye as my shyness kicked in fully feeling slightly embarrassed.

He picked up one of my story books staring at it

strangely as he read out the title " Married to the frog prince"

"What a really strange story book" he said his accent really thick and ringing in my ears.

I decided to just ignore him hoping that he'll find me weird and leave me alone. But sadly, that didn't happen.

"Are you mute? Or are you trying to ignore me?" He pressed on staring at me strangely but I just kept quiet still refusing to talk to him.

"Hmm, I doubt you're mute though. I mean who knew that the strange girl who just kissed me was my neighbor" he said his voice filled with mischief as he moved closer to me.

I refused to cave, still keeping quiet. He gave me a playful smirk as I felt him move closer to me and bent his face coming right in front of mine with his nose not that far from mine as my eyes widened in shock.

"Should we kiss again?" He whispered softly teasing me causing me to push him off me in annoyance, my cheeks really heating up as I heard him laugh out loud.

"You're a jerk!" I insulted

"So now she talks." he said still full on laughing at me causing me to glare angrily at him.

"Stop it."

"Okay. I'll stop laughing princess" he teased holding back a laugh "Don't call me that, only my dad calls me that" I warned angrily

"Alright. So, you like to read?" He asked curiously finally calming himself down as he took the seat next to me.

"Yes, do you?"

"Not really, I prefer playing video games instead." He answered.

"Are you really from America?" I asked curiously staring at his cute boyish face.

"Yes, New York actually" he replied proudly

"Wow that's my dad's favorite place in the world. He's always wanted to go there" I said awestruck by the fact that's he's from there.

"Trust me it's a really great place, New York is the city where dreams come true" he said with a smile making my tummy do little flips as I blushed shyly.

"Then why did you leave?" I asked curiously as I watched him think about it a bit.

"I don't really know. Mum says we're going to go back soon. I think she's here to sort something's out that must be important" he answered.

"And you don't know what they are?"

"Yeah, but I'm sure it's something really good because she looked happy while bringing us here" he replied.

"Okay" I answered turning my attention back to the book i was reading.

"How old are you?" He asked all of a sudden staring at me.

"I'm eight" I answered

"I'm ten. Wanna be friends?" He asked nicely holding out his hand with a smile making me smile too.

"Yes" I answered giving him my hand to shake only for him to hold it softly pulling me closely and giving me a kiss on the cheek surprising me.

"That's how we make friends in New York" he said with a shy smile on his face as i stared at him with wide eyes unable to blink, the feeling of his lips on my cheek tingly.

"Really?" I asked still surprised finally able to find my voice.

"Yes princess" he replied with a smile as I watched him pick one of my story books and busying himself with it. I didn't even realize when I started smiling already liking the brown boy with an American accent that sat next to me reading my favorite story book.

Current day,

I couldn't concentrate on anything as my mind replayed everything that went on at the restaurant and the phone call between Damolà and I. Why won't he stop trying? It's like how he was back when we were kids. Always trying to have his way and making me do things I'd never do but always having that same effect on me.

He used to use it to tease me back then and anytime he touched me or hugged me I'd go mute and my eyes will be as wide as saucers as I blushed shyly and he found it really amusing and started calling it The Damolà effect.

I disliked the name back then because it was so hard trying to hide anything from him. He could always tell when I was lying or pretending. It was like he had his own personal cheat codes when it came to me. Although little me back then loved it because he was always so attentive to me and it made me feel special. Made me believe that I was his whole world.

My thoughts were cut short by the sound of my phone ringing and picking it up to see that it was my little sister calling.

"Hey sis, what's up?" She greeted

"I'm alright, to what do I owe this call Lade?" I teased lightly making her chuckle "Can't I call my big sister again?"

"You can , I'm just curious that's all" I answered

"Well, you wouldn't believe what Tolu and I found among daddy's really old suitcases" she said sounding surprised and slightly excited.

"What's that?"

"A picture, a very old picture." She answered "What picture?" I asked confused.

"Just open your phone and check it out. I've sent it to you" she said sounding really vague before hanging up confusing me.

Opening up my phone, i saw the notification that she

had sent me something. I clicked on it and the picture loaded the content shocking me. It was a picture of Dami kissing me on the cheek while we were out in the veranda on the very first day we met.

But how? My dad saw it? And he took a picture?! How come we never saw it.

The picture wasn't really clear with some parts wearing out but both our faces were very distinctive and you could see his eyes closed as he kissed me and mine opened in total surprise.

We looked so young and seeing the innocence in the picture was about to make me cry.

I held back my tears surprised to know that my dad was actually there that day. He saw everything and he heard everything. My sister sent another picture but it was the back of the picture and what was written on it in my dad's handwriting.

05/02/2011

Daràsimi's first kiss.

I didn't even realize when a tear dropped down my face as I felt really emotional. I couldn't believe what I was seeing and before I knew it the waterworks came running down as I started to miss him so much.

A message popped up on my screen from my sister as I wiped my eyes reading the text.

Lade luv: I can't believe daddy saw a boy kiss you and took a picture of it. That's so cute. I laughed softly replying her,

Me: I didn't even know that he was there, I'm honestly so shocked. Did mummy see it?

Lade luv: of course not, we don't want her freaking out now. Besides it's a really old picture, Tolu and I decided to hide it for you. I don't think mummy has ever seen that picture. The way daddy hid it *ehn*, you wouldn't even realize it was there.

I just smiled harder remembering my dad's sneaky character.

Me: Thanks Lade. When I'm back I'll collect it from you guys.

Lade luv: Alright sis, Dara daddy really loved you. For him to have kept this. he wanted you to be happy every time and I know you miss Damolà.

Me: Lade, c'mon. It's been so long.

Lade luv: it doesn't matter, I can help you find him.

I'm sure he never forgot you. The two of you had something really special, we all could see it.

Not wanting to reveal the truth to my younger sister about meeting Damolà yet i changed the subject.

Me: it's fine Lade, I'll be fine. Don't worry. Thanks for showing me the picture.

Lade luv: Anytime sis, ttyl.

CHAPTER EIGHT

DAMOLÀ

Rain droplets fell softly outside my glass windows with the clouds dreary and gray as I sat on my couch in the living room drinking wine and listening to soft jazz play in the background. The silence in the penthouse giving me a sense of calmness and peace as my thoughts drifted to several things before finally landing on one.

My muse

She was beautiful and she was making me lose my fucking mind. My fingers itching to hold her and kiss her crazy. It was exactly like how I was when I was a kid, I could never control myself around her always wanting to touch her, hug her and kiss her even with how young I was.

Simi always had my blood pumping hot in the good way and right now it was worse and I didn't know how to feel about it or control it without scaring her away. Picking up my phone and dropping the empty glass on the table, I dialed the one person that always knew the perfect answer to most of my problems. The phone rang a while before he finally picked up.

"Hey brother!" He greeted in excitement causing me to roll my eyes.

"Hey Tom, you busy?" I asked

"At all, just chilling. why? You missing me already?" He teased playfully causing me to groan in slight annoyance at that as I heard him release a chuckle.

"Stop trying to annoy me Tom."

"Of course, so what can I help you with?" He asked sounding really interested to hear what I had to say.

"There's a girl and I like her. Like really like her but I'm not sure how to go about it because we lost contact for ten years and she doesn't want me around her" I finished trying to summarize it all for him to understand.

"Wow! This is a lot. Who's she? Do I know her?" He asked curiously

"No you don't know her but you will soon. Her name's Daràsimi"

"Really? So she's Nigerian too. Cool"

"Yeah."

"So you like this girl?" He questioned "Yes I do."

"Okay. And she doesn't want you around her?" He asked sounding slightly confused.

"Yeah. But I know she's lying and tries refusing to accept that my feelings for her are real and what she feels for me too is real" I answered.

Tom took in a deep sigh everything seeming a little bit too much to take in for him.

"Bro you know what this isn't a conversation we can have over the phone. I'm coming over"

"But it's raining" I stated

"I have a coat." And with that he hung up causing me to stare at my phone in slight shock.

"Okay." I muttered softly to myself.

In some minutes, Tom was right outside my door in his trench coat slightly damp and smelling like soft rain and smoke. His lips quirked up in an excited smile as he locked eyes with me, immediately pulling me in for a bro hug as I tried to push him off.

He just chuckled and walked in with my body slightly damp from hugging him. I watched him walk into my kitchen grabbing himself a can of Gatorade as he took a huge gulp. I sat on the kitchen stool as I leaned on the counter looking at him make himself comfortable in my penthouse.

"That was fast." I said breaking the silence.

"I was around and on a date that wasn't really going anywhere" he shrugged giving me a slight smirk.

"I'm not even going to ask"

"So who's this girl that's got your mind running miles" He asked seeming intrigued as he leaned over the counter his eyes not leaving mine.

"She's my first love" I answered my reply immediately causing him to break out into a huge grin.

"Well ain't that a surprise. Dami knows what love is" he teased

"Oh shut up Tom. But yeah we grew up together. When I went back to Nigeria with mum that's when I met her. We were neighbors" I explained

"Really?"

"Yeah, it was weird how we met actually. She took my first kiss" I said with a short laugh feeling nostalgic.

"Aww really? That's so cute!" Tom said giving me a really weird look.

"We eventually became friends afterwards, best friends actually and I slowly started to fall for her. of course she never knew but we've always had this connection and she knows it."

"Hmm, okay so you're saying this girl from your childhood is your first love and now she's back after ten years and you still like her?" He asked

"Yes Tom. But she doesn't want me around and I don't know what to do." I said with a distraught sigh.

"How did you two even get to meet again?" He asked with curious eyes.

"At the rooftop party you last took me to, I sighted her while I was performing on stage"

"No way! Wow! That's just crazy! Fate really played

its cards right because I can't believe it. You met your first love and childhood crush after ten years of being apart at a party you weren't even interested in going to" he exclaimed in shock staring at me with wide eyes.

"Yeah, I honestly couldn't believe it when I saw her. I thought I was dreaming, it felt too unreal bro" I answered

"So what now?"

"I don't know but then I really want her."

"You know what bro, don't overthink it. I'm sure something like a silver lining will pop up and you'll have an opening." he advised warmly.

"You think so?"

"I know so. Trust me." He said giving me a wide grin and a thumbs up.

"Besides what girl isn't in love with the most good looking guy I know, you're Damolà, the hottest oncologist in all of Williams's research cancer institute. There's no way your girl isn't already under the famous Damolà effect" he encouraged with a wink causing me to chuckle.

"I doubt it because she's as stubborn as a mule"

"You'll see." he replied with a knowing smirk.

"Hey there's something else I've been willing to talk to you about but it keeps on slipping outta my mind" I said deciding to bring up what happened between me and Laura.

"Okay. Hit me"

We both walked out of the kitchen entering into my living room as I watched tom pull off his damp trench coat and shoes leaving him in his collar shirt and pants. He picked up the TV remote as he randomly looked for something to watch. I sat opposite him on the sofa as I wondered how I could talk to him about it.

"The last lunch date I had with simì, I took Laura along with me because she was really curious about meeting her and also was trying to get away from Dr Frazier" I started with his eyes still stuck on the TV as he still held on to the remote.

"Okay, and?" He turned to me swiftly before returning to what he was doing.

"It was quite weird, simì didn't like it because she was obviously jealous I brought another girl on our lunch date" I said with a small smile as I remembered the events that happened between us.

"So what then made it weird?"

"Laura's behavior actually, she was overly chatty with simì for no reason and in the car while we were driving back she was so quiet it honestly worried me"

"Why? What happened?" He asked curiously finally dropping the TV remote and turning to look at me.

"I somehow confessed my feelings to simì that day and she was there and I guess that shocked her because it's not something I ever do. So I got that it must've have given her quite the shock but then in the ride back to the hospital she asked me some really strange questions" I explained as Tom listened in.

"She asked if I liked simì and I told her the truth that I did and her eyes started to tear up and it looked like she was about to cry and it was so weird because I didn't know what to do or go about the current situation. When I asked her why she was about to cry she said it was allergies but Laura isn't allergic to anything. Then she said something about how I should move on from simì and that there's many more fishes in the sea."

I finished as I stared at his slightly shocked face waiting to hear what he had to say about everything.

"Wow, I mean. I always knew she had a thing for you but I didn't think it was that bad" he muttered as I stared at him slightly confused.

"What do you mean?"

"I mean that Laura likes you bro, if not even in love with you" he said forwardly his words surprising me.

Laura couldn't be in love with me. we've been friends for so long and I don't think I'm her type of guy. I mean I'd have definitely seen the signs if she was ever interested.

"Tom c'mon, it's Laura we're talking about. She's told me countless times about how no man does it for her" I disagreed with his observations as he gave me a look.

"Yeah bro, that's because YOU do it for her. I'm not surprised though, she's always around you and tries doing girlfriend stuff for you." he answered making me stare at him in disbelief.

"Like what? Tom it honestly makes no sense"

"She cooks for you on most occasions, most of the side dishes in your fridge are from her because she knows your meal plan and how much you easily lose appetite, you guys work together, she helps you pick out your dry cleaning, she has the passcode to your penthouse, you're her number one on speed dial. C'mon do you need me to go on?" He asked giving me a knowing look every one of his observation shocking me to the core.

"I never asked her to cook for me or do all of these things, she just started one day and I guess I didn't see anything to it because we were best friends and I assumed friends help out each other" I explained.

"It's not your fault bro, you're just really blind to these things. That's why I'm so surprised about this new girl. I was starting to think you were gay" he said laughing making me pick up a pillow and fling it at him.

"Tom are you sure though? I still think it might've been because she witnessed another version of me that day and it overwhelmed her." I said refusing to believe him

He sighed before answering me "Alright Damì, how many times has Laura spent the night here?"

Well a lot but that's only because she's always drinking. And I don't know why. She never tells me the reason.

"Exactly, she likes you bro but she knows you can never see her that way and it hurts her a lot so she tries to drink away the pain and then she comes knocking on your door every time hoping that when you see her like that in such a vulnerable state you'd have a change of heart and finally remove her from the friend zone"

Tom explained as my eyes widened in realization at everything.

"I can't believe Laura likes me."

"Believe it bro, why else do you think no nurse or female doctor wants to go out with you even with how much they like you?"

"Why?"

"Because they think you and Laura are together but are keeping it low key" he replied causing me to screech in surprise.

"What?!"

Tom just shook his head at my slow witted mentality to everything. "Laura and I aren't together!"

"Well they most certainly think you guys are, I mean you always eat lunch together, your schedules are similar, she's always in your office. You never hang out with anyone else apart from her"

"That's because we're best friends!" I exclaimed in slight annoyance as he released a short laugh.

"Yeah bro, Boys and girls can't be friends and certainly not best friends. I mean take a look at you and simì."

He stated with a knowing smirk on his face and that's when it all hit me like a bucket of cold ice being dumped on my head.

Laura was in love with me and she mistook my friendliness for something completely different.

Shit!

CHAPTER NINE

DARÀSIMI

Lia and I were currently at Central Park. She promised to hang out with me and take me on a tour around New York and she decided we start with Central Park. We both sat on a bench drinking strawberry slushees with the sun shining brightly above us. The park was really nice and beautiful. Since it was fall the leaves and trees were orange colored and some fell to the ground in soft heaps.

Everything about New York was amazing and it felt unreal every time I woke up and realized where I was. Lia turned to me with a smile finally breaking the warm silence.

"So what do you think?" She asked

"I love it, it's so warm and beautiful" I gushed happily.

"Yeah I just knew that you'd like it. You know this was where my boyfriend asked me out. He planned this really cute picnic date and I honestly couldn't get over how much I loved it" she gushed happily with a grin on her lips.

"Aww Lia, that's so sweet"

"I know right. I honestly really love him" she smiled happily causing me to smile at that. She loved him. I used to love him once till he left.

I shook off all thoughts about the past as I tried to focus on the present.

"So simì did that guy from the party reach out to you?" Her question honestly throwing me off guard as I stared at her in slight surprise.

"What?" I stuttered.

"You know, that really hot singer that was talking to you. He seemed really interested in you" she said giving me a serious look.

I just took a huge gulp of my slush not knowing how to answer her questions.

"Lia I know him" I stuttered nervously but she didn't really hear me as my phone immediately dinged with a random notification.

Her eyes noticed my lock screen and her eyes flashed with something like recognition.

"Aww simì is that you?" She asked still starting at it.

"Yeah."

"Who's the boy kissing you on the cheek?" She asked in slight surprise and a smile.

"That's him."

"Who?" She asked still focused on the picture.

"The hot singer from the party." Her head immediately went up in surprise at my answer her eyes wide as saucers.

"Is he your boyfriend?!" She asked in surprise

"No, at all." I immediately replied

"Then how?"

"We grew up together. He used to be my best friend." I answered still staring at her shocked face.

"Oh wow."

"We lost contact for ten years and coincidentally met at that rooftop party" I explained as I watched her eyes widen more.

"Oh my god you're kidding!" she exclaimed

I shook my head in response to that and she just gasp still really overwhelmed.

"Ten freaking years?! And you met that night. At the party I coincidentally invited you for?"

She asked again

"Yes"

"Oh my god! This is unbelievable,really!"

"Yeah I know."

"Who saw who first?" She asked

"I think he did because he approached me first and then we started talking. I told him my name and he told me his and that's when it all came together." I answered.

"Wow, I'm honestly surprised." she said still feeling overwhelmed by the story.

"Yeah."

"So what now? Are you two keeping in touch?" She asked in keen curiosity.

"Somehow, he's invited me out on two lunch dates since that night but that's about it. He rarely calls or texts me much." I answered

"Okay. Maybe he's just really busy but then what about you? I mean what have you done to keep the connection open?" She asked giving me a slightly stern look.

"Nothing actually." I muttered turning away from her prying eyes.

"I see and why's that? Because from what I can tell he seems really interested in you. If he wasn't or wanted nothing to do with you I doubt he'd have asked you out for lunch." She stated as a matter of fact.

I gave a deep sigh to that "I know he's interested in me Lia. I'm just not interested"

"Why?" She asked softly

"Because I'm scared, Damolà and I have a special

kind of relationship and those really intense feelings I used to feel for him were too much for me to handle and eventually I got hurt in the end. Besides he's changed since the last time we met, it's been years Lia, I feel like we should just leave things the way it used to be." I answered with a distraught look on my face.

Lia stared at me as she seemed to try and figure me out. "Simì, why're you running away?"

My eyes slightly widened in surprise at her question not exactly knowing how to answer her as I held her questioning eyes. Finally finding the courage to answer her question, I put on an unbothered look "I'm not running from anything Lia. I just want things to not change"

"Then I'm kinda sorry for you sweetie because things always change whether you like it or not" she replied and finally dropped the topic causing my mind to whirl feeling conflicted about everything.

♪♪♪♪♪

Things seemed to be back to norma. I had fully begun classes and currently worked a part time job as a waitress at a coffee shop to make some additional money. Lia and I got really close and she invited me out with her into the city most nights which I really enjoyed.

Slowly her friends started to become mine and I seemed to had settled in perfectly. Ever since that weird lunch date between I and Damolà, I hadn't really heard from him and as much as I didn't want anything to do with him anymore I still craved to see him. Makes no sense, I know.

A part of me worried if he was doing fine and yearned to call him and hear his voice but another part of me thought that it was good and that this was for the better. It's been over a week since I last saw or heard from him and I considered it quite weird that he suddenly decided to stop trying. Deciding to shake off all intrusive thoughts about Damì and focus on my work, I heard the front door chime and my eyes swept up from the machine only to lock with deep black eyes.

Damì stood right in the little cafe I currently worked at looking like such a man in a grey sweatshirt and sneakers as he stood next to a smaller white skinned guy fully dressed corporate. His eyes locked with my surprised ones with a shocked and slight curious glint in them as he slowly accessed me in my uniform making me feel a bit under dressed. His friend wondered who he was staring at as he turned to look at me, I stopped what I was doing and dusting my hands on the front of my white apron as I left my position at the counter to go attend to them.

The mini cafe I worked at wasn't always that busy and we had little customers over time. The pay was okay and manageable enough for me to afford the basic necessities like groceries, bus fare, sanitary supplies and stuff. Taxi fares became too expensive for me so I had to cut my budget quite a lot and started to take the subway. We worked with shifts and I normally covered the morning shifts since most of my classes were in the late afternoon. I worked Monday's, Wednesday's and Friday's.

I watched Damì and his friend walk towards a table as they both sat down with me approaching them as I tried easing my nerves and the butterflies in my tummy.

"Hi, Good morning and welcome to Lottie's cafe, what can I get you?" I greeted formally with a small smile as I stood right in front of them.

His friend turned to meet me as I finally got a closer look at him. He was quite handsome with his facial features less than average with short dirty blonde hair, blue eyes and a nice pair of thin lips. He wasn't that bad to look at but I honestly wondered why he was dressed so proper while Damì just looked like he stepped out of a gym.

"Hi, can I get a hot cup of Americano and he'll have just black coffee with ice" he ordered nicely as I nodded my head writing down their order in a small notepad.

"Alright, I'll have your orders soon" I said about to walk away when I heard my name called stopping me from leaving.

"Simì" he called as I turned to stare at his eyes which seemed to have soften slightly at my presence.

God! I've missed him.

Damolà was the finest man I had ever seen and I didn't realize how much I had missed seeing his beautiful face until I stood right in front of him trying to ignore the feeling he gave me just by him calling my name.

"Hey. it's been a while." I muttered softly

"Yeah, I've been quite busy lately." he replied his voice sounding like music to my ears.

"Okay. it's nice to see you're okay"

"You work here?" He asked curiously

"Yeah, just started this week."

"Why?" He asked seeming confused at that.

"What do you mean?"

"You're a grad student in engineering, I don't think you're suited as a waitress simì" he said making me feel slightly insecure at that.

"Well I'm not exactly an American citizen with a green card so we can't all afford to choose."

"Simì that's not what I meant." he said with a deep sigh causing me to softly bite my lower lip the embarrassment slowly eating me up.

"Damì we can talk about this some other time, I need to go prepare your order and attend to other customers" I said in a rush walking away from his table wishing I could take those words back hoping he hadn't started to hate me already.

As I made their coffee orders I could feel Damì's eyes on me all through his stares causing me to feel some type of way. He wasn't even trying to hide the fact that he was staring and it was slowly starting to get under my skin. Picking both their orders as I walked back to their tables trying my hardest best to ignore Damì's intense stares.

"Simì right?" His friend called with a nice smile on his face.

"Yeah. Hello?" I greeted slightly confused that he was trying to talk to me as I placed their coffee right in front of them.

"Forgive my manners, I'm Tom. This grumpy bear's

best friend" he introduced politely with an outstretched hand.

I guess he was called grumpy bear quite a lot and funny enough it suited him. "Hi." I said with a smile shaking his outstretched hand.

"I'm throwing a birthday party at my penthouse in Manhattan and I want you to come." He said forwardly the same polite smile on his face his invite completely shocking me.

"A party? Me? But you don't even know me much" I said causing him to give a short laugh to that.

"Oh I know you." he muttered with a soft smirk at the corner of his lips causing me to stare at him still confused.

"You can be Damì's plus one. It's on Saturday and the style is 90's retro so make sure to come in costume okay." He said with a playful wink as I watched him pick up his coffee and stand up about to leave without even bothering to hear what I had to say in regards to his invite.

"I really have to go bro, I'm late and if I'm not at that meeting my dad's gonna kill me" he said to Damì with a playful smile on his face as I watched Damì nod softly at that a small smile on his face.

"It was really nice to meet you simì, hope to see you at my party okay." He said once more and finally took his leave as I stood still in shock at what just happened.

"When does your shift end?" Damì suddenly asked getting me out of my shocked state as I turned to look at his really smooth face.

"Why?"

"I need you to go somewhere with me." he answered simply.

"Eleven a.m." I replied.

"Alright, I'll wait." He said bringing out his phone from his pocket and making himself comfortable on his seat.

"What do you mean you'll wait? Don't you have work today? And where are you even taking me to?" I questioned as I tried to get his attention away from his phone.

"Today's my day off. I'm not doing anything right now so I have enough time to wait for you and I'm taking you somewhere" he explained sharply giving me a look that said I should drop it making me scoff in slight disbelief.

I huffed in annoyance deciding not to mind him as I went back to my station behind the counter to continue with my work.

He can wait for as long as he wants I don't care.

As I went about my work my eyes went to him and he seemed content with his coffee scrolling through his phone with air pods in his ears as he comfortably waited for me to be done with my shift. As sweet as it was I refused to let that sway me as I remembered how rude he was to me before. The end of my shift was getting near as I finished a customer's order. My side eye swept to his table once more as I saw some lady dressed in really skimpy clothes approach him.

My stomach started to slightly churn in jealousy as i watched their encounter. His lips lifted up in a small smile as he listened to what it was the lady was saying with his air pods no longer in his ears.

Is he smiling at her?! Are you kidding me?

She outstretched her tiny hand slightly grazing his and it seemed like she was openly flirting with him and he didn't even seem to mind at all. He just gave her a small smile nodding his head to whatever shit that she was spewing from her mouth. He gives me a crappy attitude all the time and now he's smiling and acting like a proper gentleman to her.

I'm not gonna stand here and watch this anymore.

I didn't even realize when I left my work station walking straight towards the both of them as I stood right in front with a frown on my face interrupting their loving moment the both of them seeming surprised at my sudden presence.

"Hi, welcome to Lottie's cafe, what can I get you?" I said almost immediately catching both their attentions.

Damì just stared at me in confusion wondering why I was suddenly taking her order and not the waiting customer at my work station.

Yeah it's just annoying to see him talk to another girl.

"Oh, Hi.I'm really good. Thank you" she said in her tiny voice waving me off but no way was I giving up that easily.

"I'm sorry but you can't sit in here without ordering anything or I'm going to ask you to leave. Sorry company policy" I replied with a fake shrug and smile as she just stared at me in disbelief.

"Excuse me?" She said giving me an incredulous look.

"You have to leave if you aren't interested in ordering anything" I repeated giving her my bravest look refusing to back down.

She just scoffed in irritation and annoyance as I watched her pick up her purse and walk out of the cafe making me smirk in victory. I finally turned away from her meeting Damì's intense eyes looking really amused by my attitude.

"When you said you were gonna wait I didn't think you'd bring in company." I said with a slight huff as I walked away from him feeling pride at how I managed to send that bitch away from him.

Soon enough I was finally done with my shift as i picked up my purse as i arranged my outfit and hair at the small locker room out back. Feeling okay with how I currently looked I walked back into the cafe, my eyes finding Damì still seated at his table. Unknowingly a smile took over my features as I happily walked towards him.

I can't believe he actually waited for me.

He noticed me fully dressed and no longer in my

uniform as I stood right in front of him. "Are you done?" He asked

"Yeah."

"Let's go then." he said as he finally got up from his seat the both of us walking out of the cafe.

CHAPTER TEN

DAMOLÀ

The ride was silent as i drove through the city of New York. She sat still in my car not saying anything or glancing at me. Taking a sharp turn making her jump in surprise at that her eyes swept to mine in annoyance making me smirk at the fact that I got a reaction out of her.

"Could you drive at least like a normal person?" She snapped

"What's wrong with my driving princess?" I said with a smirk playing dumb and wanting to push her buttons.

She just softly groaned in annoyance slightly rolling her eyes and ignoring my question. "Why're you working at that cafe simì?" I asked curiously.

"Because I need to survive and I'm not an American citizen" she answered

"But you have a work visa don't you?" I asked confused.

"Yeah, How else do you think I was able to get a job at Lottie's?"

"So you didn't try anywhere else? You just decided to accept working as a waitress?" I pushed as i watched her frown deepen.

"I wasn't accepted!" She snapped in anger "What do you mean you weren't accepted?"

"The companies I went to applying for engineering jobs declined me. They said my resume and work experience weren't up to par and I needed to have a complete certification from a major American or Ivy League university to be able to work with them. Just a simple work visa and certificates from back home in Nigeria isn't accepted here and wasn't even going to cut it." She explained with a solemn look on her face.

"Oh, I'm sorry simì. I didn't think it was like that" I answered feeling embarrassed for putting her in a spot.

"It's fine. Until I'm able to get my masters degree from NYU I can't work at any big time engineering companies or anything. I can only work meager jobs to keep myself to survive thanks to the work visa."

"I understand but I'm sure it won't be for long. I'll talk to some of my friends, I'm sure we'll figure something out" I offered politely.

"No you don't have to. I'll be fine." she immediately said trying to reject my help.

"I know you'll be fine simì but I can't just sit and watch you waste your qualifications working at some dry ass cafe when I know I can help you." I replied as I watched her sigh softly.

"If you insist then but thank you Dami" she appreciated with a smile.

"You're welcome."

I finally stopped the car in the parking lot of the luxurious apartments that I stayed in. She looked out of the window confused about where we were.

"Where is this place?" She asked

"The apartment where I live in. C'mon let's go" I answered stepping out of the car as she also did the same.

We both walked towards the elevators as I pressed the button taking us to the penthouse on the last floor of the building. The elevator stopped and we got out walking towards the door to my penthouse.

Opening up the doors with my key we stepped in and the lights turned on automatically causing her to gasp in surprise. Walking in a little further as she stood in front of me I watched her eyes move over the entire floor marveled by how luxurious it looked. Turning to look at me in delight she asked "You live here?"

"Yeah." I answered pulling off my sneakers and putting on my house slippers. Walking in to my room to get another pair for her as I met her still standing in the hallway. Dropping them on the floor, I gestured for her to take her shoes off and put them on which she did and immediately walked into the living room.

I heard her gasp in shock at how large it was as she walked closer to the glass windows staring out unto the city's view.

"Your house is amazing" she gushed in delight.

"Thanks" I replied with a small smile brimming at the sides of my lips.

Walking towards her I opened the sliding glass doors stepping out into the balcony as I watched her eyes widen in surprise at that. She immediately followed suit joining me outside as she gasped once more in amazement at the view. The sun was bright and the rays were hitting the glass doors and windows and the breeze flew past us softly grazing our faces.

"It's so beautiful up here" she said absentmindedly.

"It's why I bought the place." Her eyes widened in surprise at my remark as she turned to look at me.

"This is yours?" She asked not sure she heard me the first time.

"Yeah."

"Wow, Dami it's really impressive. You've really outdone yourself" she said in admiration making me feel a bit shy underneath her admiring eyes.

"It's nothing" I answered trying to be modest.

She just smiled at that continuing to marvel at the view of the city.

"Simì I'm really happy you're here with me" I said getting her attention as I watched her blush.

"Why did you stop calling me?" she asked.

I had no ideal reason to why I stopped calling her, I was indeed busy but there were times I just thought that I was doing too much and needed to give her space to settle down. I also needed space to figure out how real my feelings for her were and it was. My feelings didn't waiver at all.

"I was just really busy with work. A lot of surgeries happened during those weeks" I said looking away from her questioning eyes.

"Oh that must've been tiring for you."

"It's alright. We should go in" I said ending the topic and walking back into the house.

I watched her look around my living room before her eyes landed on my black guitar. It felt weird seeing her in my house and except from Laura I haven't brought any other girl in here and looking at her from where I sat looking so small in her white mini dress her fingers softly stroking my guitar at where it stood was doing things to me.

"Is this yours?" She asked softly getting me out of my dirty thoughts.

"Yes. You can pick it up if you want" I said giving her the go ahead as I stared at her drinking every inch of her body.

She picked up the guitar as she sat down on the couch placing it properly underneath her perky breasts and atop her thighs. She held it like a pro. Not with dainty fingers or trembling arms but like she knew what she was doing. And that alone was the sexiest thing I had ever seen.

"It's been a while I played the guitar. I haven't touched any ever since." she hesitated softly.

"Ever since he died." I completed the sentence watching how my words slightly hit her but she just masked it with a soft look.

"Yeah."

"You can play something if you want, I don't mind." I offered wanting to hear her play.

It's been a while I saw her hold up any musical instrument. After she lost her dad, a part of her also died and she quit playing. But as she sat right in-front of me holding up my guitar I silently wished for her to play anything.

I needed my musical muse back.

She tuned the acoustic guitar taking a deep breath before her fingers lightly brushed through the strings the sound immediately echoing through the house. Her hands were familiar with the chords and I could see how flawless she looked with it. She finally started playing and the tune seemed very familiar. Her eyes closed and her fingers moving across the Strings releasing a very sweet melody as I stared struck at her in disbelief at how amazing she was. The tune she was playing was a song her dad used to sing for her when she was little. He composed her a special song which she always sang to me every time we played together as kids boasting about how much her dad loved her to write her a song.

Looking deeply at her I saw a tear drop from the sides of her eyes as she seemed so deep in her zone playing the tune and my heart broke at the sight. Simì was missing her father and I realized that playing the guitar was opening up memories that she must've buried deep down.

The song stopped and she opened her eyes to find me staring deeply at her and that's when I saw it all. The sadness and pain in her eyes.

My muse was broken and she needed me to fix her.

CHAPTER ELEVEN

DARÀSIMI

I finished playing the tune my dad used to sing to me as a child as I finally opened my eyes to find Damolà staring deeply at me looking extremely awestruck. It suddenly hit me that he hadn't seen me play in a long time and it must've come off as a shock to him that I was still really good with playing the guitar. I felt the sides of my eyes slightly filled with tears and I immediately cleaned it off with the back of my hands not wanting him to see that I've been crying.

I wasn't going to let him see how broken I was

"Wow simì that was beautiful." He said finally seeming to get himself.

I shook off my emotions and burying them in the deepest parts of my mind wanting to seem strong and the same again.

"It's nothing, I just wanted to see how it'll feel to play the guitar again."

"You honestly shouldn't have stopped. You're good simì, maybe even better than me" he appraised with a glint in his eye slightly surprising me at the compliment.

"I doubt that. You've been playing for a long time Dami and I haven't even touched a guitar in years." I said immediately waving off his compliment.

"Doesn't matter, your dad was a musical prodigy and you have his genes."

"Dami can we please talk about something else?" I asked almost immediately cutting him short, my expression uncomfortable at the fact that he brought up my dad as he realized that I was back to my usual self.

"Okay." I replied dropping the topic.

"Dami I have to go. My classes start soon" I said checking the time on my watch wanting to escape his stares and the current tension between us.

"Oh, okay. Let me just change into something more

appropriate and I'll drop you off" He offered standing up from the couch and leaving to go to his room when I stood up and stopped him.

"No it's fine, I'll take the subway. It was nice if you to bring me here and you have a really

nice penthouse." I rushed picking up my purse and walking into the hallway with him staring at me in confusion and slight worry.

"Simì," he called lightly as I turned to look at him. "The door's locked."

"Oh, could you please open it?" I asked nicely.

"I will only on one condition." He said with folded arms causing me to look at him in slight annoyance.

"Excuse me?"

"You heard me, I'll open the door on one condition" He repeated giving me a look.

I chewed the insides of my lips before finally giving in "Okay, fine! What is it?"

"Go on a date with me" "What?"

"Tomorrow night, me and you on a date" He said

boldly asking me out. I just stared at him in disbelief unable to believe what was currently happening.

"What if I don't want to?"

"Then you don't get to leave which by the way is still a win for me" He answered giving me a sly smirk.

"So you're putting me in a spot that wouldn't allow me reject you?" I asked giving him an incredulous look.

"However way you seem to see it."

"You're crazy." I said laughing humorlessly.

"I guess you don't want to leave then" he said ignoring my remark and leaving to walk into his room when I stopped him.

"Wait!"

"Yes?" He answered seeming to love how much he was pushing my buttons.

"Fine! I'll go on a date with you." I agreed with a frown on my face feeling very defeated.

A sly smirk pulled up on his lips at my answer "Good girl"

He brought out the keys from his pockets walking into the hallway and finally opening the door for me. As

I walked out about to leave he held my hand the feeling causing my skin to prickle hot as goosebumps erupted on them.

He moved closer to me closing the gap between us as he leaned in with his breath tickling my ear.

"I'll pick you up tomorrow night princess, eight o'clock sharp. Can't wait" and with that I felt him lightly kiss the sides of my neck causing me to gasp in surprise and slight delight at that before he closed the door leaving me struck in a slight daze anticipating for tomorrow night.

♪♪♪♪♪

Sitting on my bed with clothes scattered all of over the place I was on a video call with my best friend back home discussing everything and planning what to wear on my date with Damolà tonight. My laptop sat on top an amount of clothes with Sharon talking and trying to get me to calm down.

"Sweetie, relax. Take deep breaths. Deep breaths simì" she said gently as I flopped face down on my pillows groaning in frustration.

"Why's Damolà doing this to me?!" I mumbled face down into my pillows.

"I didn't hear you clearly simì?"

Raising my head from the pillows I stared back at the screen with a pout as she softly giggled at my current situation.

"I honestly can't believe he asked you out on a date." She teased making me roll my eyes.

"What should I wear??!" I cried out

"First of all where's he even taking you to?" She asked curiously.

"I honestly don't know, he didn't say. He just said he's picking me up by eight pm." I answered.

"Okay. How about you dress causal but not too casual" she offered

"Not helping" I replied giving her a look.

Lia immediately walked into the dorm muttering a mouthful of beautiful profanities at how the room currently looked.

"Oh my goodness!, did a cloth bomb blow up in here?" She asked with wide eyes as she tried to walk around the pile of clothes thrown everywhere.

"Hi Lia" I greeted with a cheeky smile

"Simì, what's going on?"

"I have a date tonight and I'm freaking out" I answered. "You have a date? Aww" she said with a smile.

"I have nothing to wear" I cried out my best friend rolling her eyes at my antics.

"I think you have a lot to wear simì" Lia muttered quite sarcastically as she took in the state of our room.

"Help me!"

"Okay. Chill, why don't you put this on?" She said picking out a black leather mini skirt from the pile.

"That looks really nice." Sharon added over the screen

"Really? Okay what should I wear it with?" I asked staring at the both of them. "You could pair it with your white corset top?" Sharon answered.

"The lacy one?, you think it'd go with the skirt" I replied feeling a bit unsure.

"Yes it so will! And you could wear a pair of Doc martens. That's honestly really perfect" Lia answered with a grin causing Sharon to nod in agreement.

"But what if I feel chilly, the date's at night guys" I reminded.

"Don't you have a coat?" Sharon asked confused as I nodded my head in a No. "You could borrow mine, it's alright" Lia offered nicely.

"Really?"

"Yeah. I don't mind" she replied causing me to hug her in appreciation. "Thank you Lia"

She just giggled releasing me from the hug as we both stared at each other. "Now tell me simì, Who's this guy that asked you out?" She asked curiously

"Damolà. And trust me it was so out of the blue" I answered as she squealed happily.

"The hot singer?! Oh my god simi! That's so cute" she said happily sitting next to me on my bed.

"No it's not, it's annoying. He asked me out in such a way that I had no choice but to say yes" I grumbled in slight annoyance as I remembered.

Lia just stared confused at Sharon on the screen at my current attitude.

"Don't mind her Lia, she's just angry that this time

she can't run away from her feelings" Sharon explained causing Lia to nod her head in understanding.

"She totally likes him. How else would she completely turn our room upside down looking for what to wear if she wasn't interested" Lia teased with a playful smile on her face.

"Oh please Lia, I just don't want to look disgusting while on a date with him. I'm not dressing up for him" I defended causing her to give me a look.

"Well it's almost eight and you look a mess. If you wanted my advice on when to start prepping up for your date. I'd say right now" Lia advised warmly as she went towards her bed and flopped right down on it.

"Yeah you're right" I said with a soft sigh my mind whirling in circles as the date drew nearer.

"Guys I'm nervous, I don't know what might happen tonight. I'm scared." I confessed opening up to the both of them with a worrisome look on my face.

"Aww simì don't be, this is good okay. I know that you're scared of change but this change is really good for you. I'm sure you'll have a great time tonight" Lia reassured me her words warming my heart deeply.

"You really think so?"

"I know so." She answered

"Thanks."

It was finally time and the butterflies in my tummy filtered like crazy as I tried very hard to calm my raging nerves. Lia came out of the bathroom staring at me in amazement with an excited smile on my face.

"How do I look?" I asked still feeling really worried.

"You look fucking amazing! Oh my goodness simì. Dami's going to lose his balls once he sees you tonight. Wow!" She exclaimed excitedly causing me to smile shyly her compliments making me blush.

"Thanks Lia."

"Is he here already?" She asked curiously

"No he hasn't called yet" I answered

"I'm sure he's on his way. You honestly look really beautiful simì and wow I love what you did with your hair" she complimented making me smile.

"Thanks."

My phone rang almost immediately his call coming in as I took in a deep breath before finally answering it with his deep voice filling my ears.

"Hey."

"Hi."

"I'm right outside your dorm." he said simply. "I'm coming."

He ended the call as I turned to look at Lia my nerves coming back up.

"Don't sweat it babe, you'll be fine. Don't worry" she reassured me once more making me breathe in relief as I picked up my purse and slipping on my coat before finally leave the room.

CHAPTER TWELVE

DAMOLÀ

Getting out of the car and leaning on it as I waited for her to come out of her dorm. Immediately she walked out my breath got caught up in my throat and I suddenly forgot how to breathe. She looked breathtaking.

Literally!

She took classy steps towards me taking her time to slowly kill me as I stared at her legs in that mini skirt. Her makeup was so simple it was hard to tell if she was even putting it on but it honestly looked really good on her. Her black hair fell down to her shoulders in a puffy

Afro adorned with shiny hair clips styled properly. She got closer to me as I inhaled her

perfume the scent smelling so rich and yet so innocent.

"Fuck". I muttered softly my eyes heavily trained stuck in a adoring trance.

"Hey." She said softly her voice sounding a bit nervous.

I took in a huge gulp as I tried finding my voice as I locked eyes with her piercing ones. My body not in control of itself as I urged to take her into the car and fuck her crazy.

"Wow, simì. You.. you look" I stuttered still in a daze of how good she looked standing right in front of me.

A melanin goddess.

"You're fucking beautiful." I finally said finding my voice as I watched a smile softly grow on her face.

"Let's go." she said moving away from where I stood and walking into the car.

♪♪♪♪♪♪

We sat on the grass at Central Park watching a movie

on a really large screen with a few amount of people around watching too. I decided to take her to watch a nice movie at a popular outdoor cinema at the park. I laid out a really nice blanket and brought simple snacks like water, soda and popcorn. I wasn't really going all out with our first date because I wanted her to feel really comfortable with me but right now I was the one feeling uncomfortable trying to stop myself from getting a raging hard on from sitting so close to her.

"This is really nice." she said with a smile on her face seeming to enjoy our date.

"Really?" I answered almost immediately coming out of my really nasty thoughts about us.

"Yeah, I've always wanted to go to an outdoor cinema. There's something about the cool night air blowing in your face and the peace and quiet that just makes sense" she said as she pulled off her coat and trying to make herself really comfortable.

"I'm glad you like it. I was hoping it wasn't too boring for a first date." I said staring deeply into her beautiful eyes.

"It's perfect" she whispered with eyes still locked on mine.

My eyes slowly went down to her glossy lips and

I itched to get a taste, a feel. My body slowly moving closer to hers. She could feel the heat too and the intense attraction between us as I felt her fingers graze mine on the blanket. The movie playing suddenly seemed so distant and all I could hear, all I wanted to feel at that moment was simi's lips on mine. Our faces inched closer and I feared what I was about to do. If I kissed her, I'd want more. I won't stop.

And I could tell she wouldn't either.

Not waiting any longer I closed the gap between us kissing her deeply the feel of her lips going straight to my groin. I felt her sigh in delight at how perfect our lips were moving in sync. I wasn't just kissing her, I was making love to her lips and it was extremely amazing. The taste of her starting to be so addictive it took everything for me to redraw from her lips to give us space to finally breathe. My hands were still softly wrapped around her neck our eyes heavily locked on each other as we both took slow pants.

My God I was starting to lose my mind as I stared into those eyes.

She smiled happily before kissing me once more and I didn't realize how much I loved seeing that smile until it was a mere inch away from my face. She redrew from my lips, hers merely swollen as I watched her wipe mine with her fingers a playful smile on her face.

"You have a little bit of gloss." she whispered.

Smiling I took her hand in mine "Wanna get out of here?" I asked.

"Where?"

"You'll see princess." I said dragging her out of the open cinema.

We stood right outside Central Park holding hands with her small ones fitting just right in mine as we both smiled in excitement.

"Ever been to time's square princess?" I asked curiously and she nodded no to my answer.

I smiled to that, softly pushing her into the car as I got in and started it up and driving us to Times Square.

We were in Times Square and having a lot of fun. She was feeling so free with me and I was enjoying myself too. She was so marveled by everything and wanted to try out every activity that was happening there. So far I had taken her tons of pictures and she forcefully made me take funny selfies with her. Everything was perfect and our first date was amazing but I was just getting started. A band was currently performing and she stood right in front of them cheering them on and having fun. I took her hands in mine standing next to her and closing our mouths in a really enticing kiss.

"So what do you think about tonight princess?" I asked

"It's the best, I love it Dami." She grinned happily.

"I think I know what would make you love it more." I said with a playful smirk on my lips. "What's that?"

"A song." I answered as I left her side and walked towards the playing band.

She just watched me confusion etched on her face as I discussed quietly with the lead singer if I could join in their performance. He immediately agreed happily as we picked a song before he joined me on stage. I picked up one of their guitars as I took my stance in front of the mic as I saw her eyes widen in shock at what I was about to do. Licking my lips mischievously, I gave her a wink as she blushed at that. "This is for you princess.."

Sending the band a signal, the drummer started an upbeat bringing me in and I decided to sing a really upbeat song for her. The lead guitarist played in the intro for the song "Shut up and Dance" by walk the moon and almost immediately everyone around crowded us as

I started to sing. Staring only at an excited simì I sang my heart out as we locked eyes with the guitar in my hands as I enjoyed myself playing and having fun with the band. The band was amazing and they carried me along just fine.

I got to the chorus and everyone started dancing happily including simì as she cheered on loudly her phone in front of her as she recorded everything.

The song was slowly starting to end and the band had a blast playing the upbeat song with such precision as I carried along the excited crowd that watched us. I sang the chorus once more causing cheers to erupt as everyone sang along in happiness before finally ending the song.

Almost immediately simì ran towards me pulling me in for a hug letting out an excited laugh. "Oh my gosh Dami that was amazing!"

"Yeah I had fun."

The band mates finally came to me congratulating me and saying how impressive I was and offered for me to join their band which I politely refused.

"You're really good and I loved every moment"

"Me too princess and is it just me or I don't want

tonight to end?" I said holding her really close to me with a smile on my face.

She giggled lightly "I don't want it either."

"Well wanna go to my place?" I offered.

I saw her eyes widen in surprise at my request, before answering me. "Another time Dami, I have workshop tomorrow"

"I'll hold you to it princess." I said giving her a peck on the forehead as I held her close to me.

CHAPTER THIRTEEN

DARÀSIMI

My date with Damolà was extremely amazing and I had a really nice time. As much as I wanted to go home with him, I had to take things slow. There was still a lot of things we hadn't sorted out yet plus i had a class the next day. Currently I was at work and I had just recently started my shift. There weren't that many customers and I was becoming bored of watching the sports channel that was playing on the small TV that hung on the wall of the cafe.

Picking up my phone I decided to call Dami and hear his voice. Ever since that really wonderful date between us my relationship with him changed. We fought less, we joked more and seemed closer than before. Even with how scared I was about my feelings for him I still loved hanging around him and talking to him. He called most of the time and his rude and snappy character reduced quite a lot. We've become really comfortable around each other.

His phone rang for a while before he finally picked up.

"Hey princess" he greeted his deep voice rumbling over the p hone.

"It's simì to you." I snapped playfully.

"I'm sorry, I didn't quite catch that princess" he said his voice having a playful edge to it.

Groaning play fully I answered him "You're just really annoying dami"

He laughed at that is laugh sounding beautiful to my ears. "Are you at work?" "Yeah but I'm so bored. We currently have no customers." I answered.

"I'd have shown up but I have a really scary surgery in like ten minutes." He replied sounding apologetic.

"Oh really? What surgery?" I asked curiously and slightly worried.

"A brain surgery. One of my patients has a small

tumor at the left side of his brain so I'm going to be assisting one of the top brain surgeons in the hospital for this surgery" he explained seriously.

"Oh wow, I really shouldn't be talking to you right now so you can properly prepare for it." I suggested nicely.

"So what now? You're gonna go off?" He demanded.

"I really don't want to be a distraction to you".

"You're not a distraction simì, I love the fact that you called me. Hearing your voice right now brightened up my day" he cut in almost immediately his words making me blush shyly.

"Really?"

"Really simì, please princess, don't go." he pleaded over the phone.

"I won't go anywhere." I replied.

"Good girl."

I was about to ask him if he was free for lunch so we could meet up when I heard a female voice over the phone.

"Hey grumpy pants, let's go. We're needed in the surgical room right now!"

"I've begged you so many times to stop calling me that" he said his voice sounding slightly annoyed.

"Whatever, let's go!" The woman in the background ordered firmly.

He sighed tiredly "Princess, I currently have to go. We'll talk later I promise"

"It's okay Dami, good luck with the surgery" I said softly.

"Thanks simi" and with that he ended the call.

♪♪♪♪♪

Ten Years ago....

"Simi come to the kitchen. Your food is ready" My Mum called as I left my room in a haste my tummy rumbling as my mouth slightly watered at the delicious smell coming out of the kitchen.

Walking into the kitchen to find my dad and mum dancing playfully with no music as she blushed happily with my dad's hands on her waist as he sang softly in her ears the both of them in their own world not minding my presence. The swelling on the sides of my dad's neck had gone down with a brown plaster covering the spot where he had the surgery to take out the tumor. He looked so happy and in love with his eyes sparkling with glee as he twirled her around with my mum laughing softly.

They looked so content and happy together, I didn't realize I had been standing for long admiring the both of them as my food just stayed still on the shelf.

My mum finally noticed me and looked surprised at how I stood still and hadn't rushed out yet with my plate of food. "Simi aren't you hungry again?" She asked looking slightly confused at my current behavior. My dad finally sensing my presence released my mum from his hold as he turned to meet my eyes with a smile on his face. "What happened princess?" He asked softly

"Dad when I grow up I'm going to marry a man just like you!" I blurted out in excitement as I watched my dad's smile widen at my statement before he bursts into a deep laugh.

"Simi stop that!, you're too young to be thinking about getting married" my mum scolded almost immediately making my dad laugh softly as he pulled me closer to him and bent right in front of me our gazes on each other. I gave him a childish pout upset at how my mum scolded me and he nodded his head playfully in understanding giving my forehead a kiss.

"Honey she's not that young to tell how true love really looks like. Princess if you ever find a man who loves you the same way I love you and treats you right just like a queen and like how I treat your mum then don't ever let him go" he advised warmly with my mum giving us both scolding looks.

"I won't dad. You're my hero and I love you" I said with a happy smile on my face as I gave him a bear hug before picking up my plate of food and walking out of the kitchen before I could hear him say those words back.

"I love you too princess" Always......

Damolà and I sat on the bed in his room as we played toys. He wouldn't stop chattering on about something but my mind wasn't listening as my thoughts wandered far off remembering how my parents looked so happy and in love dancing in the kitchen and deep down I secretly wished for something like that. A love so true and beautiful like theirs with someone to whisper sweet nothing's into my ears, make me feel special and stare lovingly into my eyes. Ten year old me desperately wanted my parents kind of love.

"Simi! Simi! Are you listening to me?"

Dami's voice snapped me out of my daydream as I turned to look at him stare at me with a disapproving frown on his face clearly not impressed with how I was ignoring him.

"I'm sorry, I was just thinking about something"

"What's that?" He asked curiously dropping down his stack of LEGO's on the floor.

"My parents. I saw them dancing together in the kitchen so happily with no music playing and I just loved looking at them. It was so romantic" I gushed happily as I told him about it as he stared at me weirdly.

"Eww, you saw your parents being mushy. That's weird princess" he mocked childishly as I glared at him.

"No it's not, it's beautiful. My dad is the best guy to my mum and when I grow up I'm going to marry someone like him" I argued back with folded arms.

"No you're not bcause you'll be getting married to me." He said seriously making me scrunch up my nose in slight annoyance.

"No way, I can't get married to you." I said

"Why? What's wrong with me?" He asked

"Nothing, I just don't love you that way. You're my friend" I answered.

His eyes looked slightly hurt at my reply before he masked it with an uninterested look and suddenly going quiet worrying me quite a bit.

"Dami are you upset with me?" I asked softly as I watched him play with his LEGO's no longer talking to me.

"Maybe"

"Why?"

"Because you said you don't love me and won't marry me." He replied turning to look at me with an emotion in his eyes leaving me struck.

"But you don't want to marry me." I muttered confused.

"Who said I didn't?" He asked

"People who get married are usually in love with each other Dami" I explained trying to get him to understand.

"I know."

"And you don't."

"I do princess, I love you." He said softly leaving me speechless and surprised as I watched him pick up his lego's and leave his room as I tried to get myself the words he spoke ringing in my ears.

He loves me.

CHAPTER FOURTEEN

DAMOLÀ

Tom's penthouse was bubbling with flashy lights with people chattering with one another holding champagne glasses in one hand as they filtered about the house in their 90's costume with loud music playing in the background. Laura stood next to me in her costume not doing much to cover up her body but she still looked good with it as we both softly gossiped about majority of tom's guest as our own way of having fun.

"Oh god look at Tessa. What exactly is she wearing? She looks like a clown." Laura mocked with a snicker gesturing to one of Tom's old college mate as she stood next to him unable to keep her hands of him.

I just snickered at that hoping my best friend realized that she just wanted to sleep with him and spend his trust fund money. My phone beeped with a text message from Simi notifying me that she was currently at the party. I smiled excitedly as my eyes searched the entire house for a glimpse of her as I couldn't wait to meet her.

Slowly she walked through the front doors my eyes immediately finding hers as I stood stunned and admiring how she looked. She looked beautiful in her costume and it was so simple but yet so jaw breaking as I noticed heads starting to turn in amazement at how good she looked as she walked fully into the party stealing the spotlight. Her outfit choice a high waist jean shorts with a neon colored crop top which was so snug on her body showing off her full perky breasts and belly button with thigh leather boots. Her Afro hair fell down to her shoulders in a full puff adorned with rainbow colored hair clips. Her makeup was so pretty and vibrant. She had on rainbow glitter on her eyes and the sides of her neck. Her lips were glossy and shimmered brightly in the lights. Her eyes found me and an excited smile immediately grew on her lips as she walked towards me.

Finally, she stood in front of me and I got a whiff of her perfume and she smelled so good, so soft. So pretty.

"Hey princess." I greeted with a teasing smirk on my

face my eyes still fully checking her out trying my very best not to get a boner as my eyes wandered down to her killer legs.

"Damolà hi." she said softly looking slightly shy to stare at me making my smile widen at that.

I haven't seen her since our date and I missed her a lot and itched to kiss her. Laura finally looked up from her phone realizing that Simi stood right in front of us. I noticed her warm expression immediately change her eyes flashing jealously as she checked her out.

"You look amazing princess"

"Thanks." she replied softly with a blush.

Her eyes finally noticed Laura who stood next to me as she offered her a polite smile. "Hey Laura, you look really nice."

Laura just offered her a passive smile "Thanks".

"So where's the birthday boy? I'm in his house, the least I could do is say hi and probably congratulate him or something." she said with a playful smile as she looked around.

I just took a sip of my champagne as I answered her

"He's probably getting banged somewhere with a chick, I haven't really gotten a hold of him since I arrived."

"Oh okay maybe later then." she said her eyes looking slightly surprised at my words.

"Where did you get your makeup done Simi?" Laura asked all of a sudden her jealous eyes staring really hard at Simi.

"My roommate did it for me. She's really good with makeup"

"Yeah right." Laura said sarcastically her weird behavior confusing Simi.

Taking a deep breath and realizing why Laura was acting weird, I didn't want her to say anything stupid to Simi and get her to feel bad so I took her hand slightly surprising her at that wanting to take her away from Laura's negative energy.

"Come with me princess."

"Where are we going?" She muttered softly as she trailed behind me my hands still holding her small ones.

"Somewhere no one gets to bother us" I smirked giving her a wink making her smile widen at that.

Opening the door to Tom's bedroom with the key he

gave me which was off limits to the guests, the both of us walked in as I turned on the lights. Taking my seat on his bed I let my eyes slowly roam down her entire body as she stood shyly by the front door.

"Princess what're you doing to me?" I groaned softly with lust in my voice as we gazed into each other's eyes. She broke eye contact and moved closer to the glass doors that lead to the balcony opening it and stepping out.

I followed suit not wanting to stay far away from her, wanting her close to me as possible.

The view was amazing with the city lights glimmering and shining brightly and the breeze blowing softly in our faces.

"Nothing ever beats the view of New York City at night" she said with a smile breaking the silence as her eyes stared ahead.

Suddenly we heard grunts and soft moans coming from the opposite balcony as we both caught the silhouette of a couple really going at it right in their balcony. Her eyes immediately widened at that as she turned quickly away from the wild scene, her expressions causing me to burst out laughing.

"Welcome to New York princess." I teased still snickering softly.

"My god people over here are crazy" she said still in slight shock an amused smile growing on the sides of her lips.

"Yeah well everyone's a little bit crazy princess. Even you."

She gave me a defensive look "I'm not crazy Damì. Nothing ever shakes me, I'm very collected when it comes to my emotions".

A sly smirk grew on the sides of my lips at her statement wanting to prove her wrong. Turning my eyes to meet hers i took a small step towards her figure.

"Really princess?"

"Yes." She muttered holding my gaze.

"Even if, I touched you.. kissed you.. it wouldn't affect you?" I whispered softly taking another small step towards her.

Her eyes shone brightly in the night a mixture of lust flickering in them as we held each other's gazes.

"It won't Damì." She replied her breathing starting to uneven.

I licked my lower lip unconsciously refusing to back down as I took another small step and this time we stood really close to each other my face an inch from hers as she looked up at me.

"What if I trailed baby kisses down your neck princess? Tiny ones. and I don't stop until I'm softly sucking your collar bone.. would that not make you a tiny bit crazy?" I whispered softly slowly leaning in to kiss her, to feel those glossy lips on mine. I could see how much my words was affecting her, how much she wanted this.

"How about we put it to a test and you see for yourself how much it wouldn't affect me." She pushed trying to act stubborn.

I lifted up my thumb trailing it over her bottom lip not breaking eye contact a soft smirk on my lips. "You know what I think princess, I think you know that you're such a bad liar" I said as I leaned to kiss her my lips softly moving with hers as i felt her moan in delight at that my lips curling up in a quick smirk at that as I continued to kiss her.

Her hands left her sides going up to hold my face pulling me closer to her as the kiss became really heated. Trailing my tongue on her bottom lip, tasting her, enjoying how sweet she felt against my mouth I felt her moan softly opening her mouth more as we kissed like as if our lives depended on it none of us wanting to let go. My hands went down to her waist as I wrapped them around her strongly and lifting her on top my body as we continued kissing with her legs wrapping around me causing me to growl in delight as I felt myself start to get hard.

"Princess you're killing me." I groaned, my voice rough as we stared into each other's eyes.

She smiled sweetly before I felt her lean into my ear as she whispered softly "Maybe you should learn not to push me then."

I smirked at that loving what was happening and loving the fact that she was being confident as she tried to hold the power in her hand.

My sweet princess if you keep on playing with fire you just might get burned.

Still carrying her i pushed her to the wall her legs strongly wrapped around my waist as I cornered her. I trailed soft kisses down her neck slightly sucking and tasting her collarbone causing her to whimper softly as we both stared at each other with raw passion in our eyes.

"Do you want to get fucked princess? Because if you don't stop being such a bad girl I might just go crazy and fuck you against this wall" I said with raw passion the lust sounding deeply in my voice.

Her eyes widened at my statement finally seeming to realize that I was serious. I could see her calculating eyes on me trying to figure out exactly what she wanted.

The tension started to relax as I felt her take in a deep breath. She released herself from my hold getting down from my body as she walked into the room away from me with no words said causing me to groan in slight annoyance at that realizing that she was trying to run away again.

"Simì stop, c'mon."

"Dami I can't do this with you, this is getting too much and I can't handle it" she said with slight fear in her eyes.

"Princess look I'm sorry about what I said out there okay. I just lost control because something about you just drives me insane that I lose fuck on what I'm saying. I didn't mean to frighten you baby." I apologized my voice tone softening as I tried to get her to understand.

"It's not that dami, it's this. It's us. We're wrong for each other" she rushed out her words hurting me to the core.

"What do you mean that we're wrong? Why do you always say things like this simì?" I asked with a pained expression on my face.

"Because it's true! Because it's real! And I'm trying to save us a lot of heartbreak in the near future" she snapped her breathing coming out in short pants the emotions in her eyes filled with raw pain.

I could see it. Clearly.

"We're not wrong princess, we fit so well. Stop trying to run away from this and just give us a chance. If it's about what I said out there then I'm sorry. I just lost control baby."

Please just give us a chance. Give me a chance princess.

She relaxed her breathing becoming even as I she sat back on the bed.

"I'm not upset about what you said out there dami" she said turning to look at me.

"Then why didn't you say anything?"

"I was just scared. Everything's moving so fast, changing so fast and I can't catch up. I felt like I was sinking." She answered honestly holding my gaze as I watched her walls slowly start to break.

"It's fine princess, I feel like that too. I mean it's not been that long since we met and I can't stop thinking about you" I confessed softly as she smiled softly at that.

"I'm not sure on what to do Dami. At one point you make me feel so different, so alive and those intense feelings scare me. What we have scares me and makes me want to run away from it." She confessed honestly making my eyes widen in slight surprise.

Was she admitting that she had feelings for me?

I realized that I was staring silently at her and I gave a fake cough averting my eyes from hers trying to process her words.

"What do you want me to do then princess? I can't help but feel what I feel for you."

"I know but how about we start off slow." She suggested.

Hmm.. I could do that.

"If that's what you want. We'll start off slow then." I said agreeing with her causing her to crack a small smile at that.

She stood up from the bed as she walked towards me taking my hands in hers as she smiled shyly at me inter-twining our hands as she gave me a soft kiss .

"Let's go down to the party i wanna dance with you" She whispered pulling me with her as I trailed after her back down into the house.

The both of us swayed happily to the music holding her really close to me as she softly grounded on my body with her being really light on her feet. I was loving her been so close to me as I could hear her breathe soft breaths with her arms around my neck as I leaned in to her neck kissing her softly and inhaling her sweet scent and loving how full her Afro hair fell out on her shoulders.

She was a fucking goddess and I was marveling at that.

"You're an amazing dancer simì" I complimented proudly my fingers softly trailing patterns on her exposed lower back.

"Of course I am. Have you forgotten how I used to perform those little dance numbers for you?" She teased with an amused glint in her eyes making me chuckle softly.

"Yeah, I never forgot how I loved watching you dance" I replied.

"Hmm it always made me feel so special you know. So confident in myself."

"That's because everything you do is amazing." I complimented as she blushed shyly averting her eyes from mine.

♪♪♪♪♪♪

Simì and I sat together talking and laughing about old memories from our childhood as she brought up so many stories that I had forgotten. The party had died down and most of the guests had left leaving a few. Tom and Laura sat opposite us with simì humoring him with the old stories while Laura just scrolled through her phone acting uninterested to what was currently going on. I liked the fact that she was no longer acting uncomfortable with me anymore. The party eventually died down and most of the guests had finally left.

So far, it was just Simì, Tom, Laura and I that were left.

"Oh my, so you're saying that Dami announced to the whole neighborhood that you guys were married?!" Tom asked sounding really amused as simì nodded her head in answer to his question causing him to immediately burst out laughing.

"Shut up bro" I said giving his head a slight hit.

"No way, like I can't believe you were such a funny and cute asshole as a kid. I always imagined you were extremely grumpy and easily got aggravated at everything" Tom listed seeming a bit surprised at the childhood stories.

"Dami? Grumpy? Nah. He rarely got angry at anyone. He was actually the nicest kid back then." Simì answered giving me a soft smile.

"Aww bro." Tom cooed softly causing me to roll my eyes at that.

"I'm surprised about this his new behavior also. I never imagined he'd grow up so different" Simì confessed as we locked gazes.

"Well princess life changes people. Dami grew up" Laura immediately cut in her tone sounding really mocking.

"I know that Laura and I changed too." She replied giving her a passive look.

"Laura just keep shut, simì's right. Dami needs to

go for behavioral therapy" Tom teased easing the thick tension in the air as he gave a snicker at his words.

I just groaned in slight annoyance as I tried to tackle him as Simì just laughed softly at our current situation.

"Tom this was a lovely party but I really should get going." She said as she stood up from the couch. "I'll drive you back to your dorm." I offered immediately getting up on my feet.

"Oh it's fine Dami, I already ordered an Uber and it's here" she replied politely refusing my offer. "Oh okay. Well let me see you off to the car" I insisted as she gave me a soft smile.

"Alright. Tom I really had fun tonight, thanks for inviting me" she said giving him a side hug as I watched him smile nicely at her.

"You're welcome anytime simì, hoping to see you again" he winked teasingly at her making her laugh softly at that.

"Same Tom. Bye Laura." She said finally acknowledging Laura who just gave her an uninterested look.

I walked her out as we both finally stood at the pavement with her Uber ride waiting patiently for us to be done talking.

"I loved seeing you here tonight simì and I really want to try with you"

"I really enjoyed myself tonight dami. Thanks for everything." She smiled softly rising on her tippy toes and giving me a peck on the cheek making me feel warm inside.

"Goodnight princess." I said softly.

"Goodnight my prince" she whispered gently with a giggle as I watched her walk into the car before finally driving off.

She called me her prince.

My eyes widened in realization as her words rang in my ears. That was the secret nickname she used to call me back when we were kids. A smile grew on my face as I realized that I was getting somewhere with her.

Simì was willing to give me a chance and I wasn't going to fucking waste it.

CHAPTER FIFTEEN

DARÀSIMI

Lia and I were chilling together as we played scrabble and talked about random stuff. I didn't have a class today and I was back from my morning shift at the cafe. Lia has been the best roommate I could've ever gotten. She's nice and sweet, very beautiful, funny and such a caring soul. We rarely have fights and when we argue it gets sorted out almost immediately.

Since we both had nothing too special to do today, I suggested we played scrabble and it's been really fun. My phone rang suddenly as it slightly startled me from the game we currently played. The screen flashing and showing Damolà's name. A smile slowly grew on my face as I couldn't suddenly wait to speak to him and picking up the call. Ever since that night at Tom's party, I felt that intense connection with him and I loved what we had. I've not forgotten how he hurt me in the past but I still want to try with him and see where this leads.

I like Dami and I like how he makes me feel all hot and warm inside, I like how he makes my skin jump and tingle with just one touch. I like how he calls me princess and stares at me as if I only existed to him. I like how he refuses to give up and I like how much that pushes me to try too.

"Hey princess" his voice sounding good filling up my ears and making me smile harder.

"Hi Dami"

"How're you?"

"I'm fine. How're you?" I asked

"Chill. Are you free this evening?" He asked

"Yeah, why?" I asked curiously picking up a piece of the scrabble blocks.

"I'm playing at a downtown jazz club tonight and I was wondering if you'd like to come and watch me perform" he asked sounding a bit shy.

"Really? Aww dami I'd love to." I replied with excitement in my voice.

"Thanks. Can't wait to see you princess, I've missed you."

He missed me...

"Me too Dami" I said shyly with warm cheeks.

I heard him chuckle in the background "So what song do you want me to sing tonight?"

"You're letting me pick?!" I asked feeling really incredulous at his question.

"Yes."

"But why?" I asked slightly confused.

"That's because you're my muse."

I'm his muse?.. that can't be true..

"You can't be serious about that dami" I said still feeling incredulous at his words. "I am simì. Very serious. You're my muse."

He insisted sounding really serious over the phone. "Wow, I didn't. I really didn't think."

"It's fine princess there's no need to get tongue tied" he teased lightly making me laugh softly.

"Tch, I'm not tongue tied dummy. Just surprised. I mean since when was I ever your muse?" I asked curiously.

"Not telling princess but you really do inspire me and I really need you to pick out the song I should sing tonight"

"Wow okay. How about You're still the one" I suggested. "By Shania Twain." He answered.

"Yeah. It's my favorite song." I gently whispered.

"I know. And I love it. I'm singing it tonight. Thanks princess"

"You're welcome dami. So I guess I'll see you tonight?"

"Yeah, I'll text you the address of the place."

"Alright. Bye Dami"

"Bye princess"

♪♪♪♪♪♪

The jazz club was buzzing with soft music playing in the background as simple looking people filtered around the place. The ambience was really nice, with soft and warm lighting, pretty looking wooden furniture and tiled marble floors. I stood at the bar in my white halter neck short dress with shiny black flats as I waited for dami. As I stood patiently waiting for him I felt the presence of someone creeping up on me and before I could turn away large hands snaked around my waist and pulling me to a body that smelled so clean and fresh. So manly.

"Hey princess" his voice sounded in my ear as I felt him lean closer into my neck subtly smelling me causing me to smile excitedly knowing who that voice belonged to.

"Hey Dami, am I late?" I asked with a playful edge to my voice.

I felt him kiss my earlobe softly the feeling causing my skin to tingle hot with the excited smile not leaving my face.

"You're right on time baby" he whispered softly causing me to giggle softly as I turned to look at him finally releasing myself from his hold.

Our eyes locked on each other with the sides of his lips curling up into a smile at my presence.

"You never fail to amaze me with your beauty

princess" he complimented as I watched his eyes slowly check me out.

"Thanks dami" I replied with a blush.

"C'mon, let me show you to your seat. I managed to steal you a front row seat so you can watch me with no problems or disturbances" he offered politely making my heart feel warm.

"Aww dami you really didn't have to."

"Of course I do, I can't let my muse sit somewhere far from me." He teased with a wink making me laugh softly at that.

"Yeah right."

We found a seat as we both sat down his eyes not leaving mine for one second. "How have you been simì?" He asked curiously.

"Quite fine, My classes hasn't been easy though plus work has been a hassle these days" I answered with a slightly tired sigh.

"Aww baby, I'm so sorry everything's been rough. Soon it'll all be better" he encouraged giving me a small smile.

"Thanks D. So when do you perform?" I asked curiously.

"In about an hour. Why?"

"Just curious to know if I'll have your full attention until then" I answered feeling quite shy to look him in the eyes.

"C'mon princess you'll always have my full attention." He replied softly taking my small hands in his with a small smile on his lips.

I bit my lip shyly trying hard not to smile with his presence and actions doing a lot of things to my body.

"I feel like we both missed out on a lot of things together while we were apart" I suddenly said getting his attention.

"Yeah you're not wrong. That's why we're going to catch up on every single one."

"How do you mean?" I asked giving him a slightly confused look.

"We're gonna play a truth game. We'll ask each other questions about anything and then we have to answer it truthfully. It's a great way to catch up." he suggested

"Hmm, I'm fine with playing. So you wanna go first?" I offered

"Yeah sure. Simì, what do you really think of me?" He asked suddenly his question taking me by surprise.

"Oh wow going straight to the point" I chuckled feeling a bit overwhelmed as he stared at me awaiting my answer.

I took in a deep breath as I answered him "Well I think you're just a stubborn good looking guy that never gives up on getting what he wants"

His lips curled up into a teasing smirk "Did you just call me good looking princess?"

"Is that the only thing you heard from what I just said?!" I asked in disbelief trying not to laugh. "Hmm yeah. I heard mostly good looking" he teased making me laugh softly.

"You're impossible"

"Your turn princess"

"Okay. Have you and Laura ever dated each other?" I asked curiously.

His face immediately morphed into a horrifying look

at my question making me wonder if I might've gone too far.

"What?! No! No way!" He exclaimed almost suddenly making me slightly jump.

"Really?" I asked once more staring closely at him.

"Really. We're just friends, that's it." He replied with so much force in his voice.

"Okay. I just thought that you two had something with how close you guys seemed" I explained.

"We are close but I just don't see her that way. I've never been attracted to her before" he replied honestly his answer causing me to unknowingly smile.

"Alright, just wanted to be sure that's all."

"Okay. My turn. Simì, did you ever date anyone?" He asked curiously staring at me intensely waiting for my answer.

Chewing my bottom lip nervously I answered him

"Yeah, I've had boyfriends"

"How many?" He asked once more.

"Just two." I answered

"I see. Did you ever love them?" He asked again with a blank expression on his face.

"You've already asked too many questions dami" I said trying to avoid his questions and prying eyes.

He raised an eyebrow to that, giving a slight shrug finally deciding to drop the topic.

"Did you ever date anyone?" I asked throwing back the question at him extremely curious to know the answer.

He raised his eyes to meet mine my knees buckling in anticipation as I waited to hear his answer.

"No simi i've never dated anyone."

His answer completely shocked me and I didn't even realize when I let out a surprised gasp to that.

It didn't seem real. Damolà has never been in a relationship. But how's that even possible?

"You're joking." I muttered.

"I'm serious princess."

"How's that even possible? You're Damolà and good looking too. I don't understand" I exclaimed in shock.

He chuckled to that "Calling me good looking again

princess, I'm starting to believe that you really fancy my looks darling" he teased with a smirk.

"Shut up dami. I'm just really surprised that you've never had a girlfriend before" I defended.

"Hmm.. I guess no girl ever interested me enough to get into a relationship with" he answered so simply with no much importance to the issue.

"Wow but I know for sure you're definitely not a Virgin" I mistakenly muttered out loud.

Almost immediately I realized I said my thoughts out loud extremely nervous to look him in the eyes with the sudden silence on our table killing me inside. Suddenly I felt him lean in closely with both of his arms on the table before I heard him speak.

"Now princess, I'd like to understand the sudden interest in my sex life"

I could literally hear the smirk in his voice and I've never been so embarrassed in my entire life to look at someone. I mustered up the little courage I had left as I raised my eyes to meet his feigning boldness.

"It's not interest dami, it was just a curious thought. You're a grown man so I just assumed you'd have had your fair share of fun"

His smirk widened at my words as he raised a questioning eyebrow to that. "Oh really princess"

"Yeah." I answered.

He just laughed to that slightly nodding his head in amusement at me.

"Well you're not wrong princess, I've had my fair share of fun and definitely not a Virgin" He said whispering the last part lowly and sounding slightly seductive.

"I figured" I said with a huff.

The smirk hadn't left his lips yet and I could just tell we weren't done yet. "Hmm are you jealous princess?"

"Jealous? Me? Why would I be?" I scoffed in slight disbelief at his question. Oh I was indeed really jealous

"I don't know but you really don't have to be sweetie. I'm always going to be here just incase you want to have your fair share of fun" he offered teasingly making me slightly choke on air as my mind made up crazy scenarios of us fucking on his bed with his offer sounding really tempting.

"You're gonna have to try harder than that if you're ever trying to get me in your bed." Why the fuck would I say that?! Where's all these confidence coming from?.

He just smiled softly saying nothing to my jabs as I silently thanked my stars because I wasn't ready to deal with a conversation like this if it headed south.

"I think it's time I went up on stage" he said bringing me out of my thoughts. Have we really been talking for over an hour? Wow.

"Oh okay. I can't wait to see you perform Dami" I said nicely offering him an encouraging smile.

"Thanks princess, I'll be back soon" he answered returning the smile as I watched him get up and walk towards the musicians on stage.

It wasn't that long before the band took their position on stage in front of their various instruments as I watched dami move towards the center stage with his acoustic guitar in his hands. His hands adjusted the mic on the stand as I watched him hold his guitar properly.

"Good evening everyone, I'm Damolà and it's a pleasure to be performing on here for you guys. I really appreciate it. I'll be singing a cover to a very popular song. This song is dedicated to someone really special to me, I hope it touches her heart." He spoke into the mic with a warm smile on his face as he turned to meet my eyes.

I couldn't help the blush that rose to my cheeks as

I smiled brightly at him. The crowd applauded softly at his introduction awaiting his performance. The band immediately played the intro with the music filling up the entire bar as I watched Dami close his eyes and smile happily as the tune wafted in the air. Strumming his guitar he joined in with the instrumentals as the song started getting better as I admired him on stage.

The intro ended and his deep voice echoed beautifully through the speakers as he sang softly. I immediately melted at that admiring how amazing he seemed singing on stage with his fingers softly strumming his guitar.

He was singing to me. His eyes finding mine filled with an indescribable emotion in them making my heart swell. He sang my favorite song so softly in front of these people but I knew that he was singing it just to me because it was now our song.

The song ended and I didn't realize that I was slightly tearing up. Dami was amazing up there, he seemed so peaceful and happy making me remember how my dad used to look whenever he played his guitar. The loud applauds from the crowd immediately snapped me out of my thoughts and I joined in clapping excitedly because that was a very beautiful performance.

He took a small bow before giving me a wink a

contented smile on his face as I returned back the smile. Damolà didn't realize that his performance just unlocked something in me. The thing I thought I had buried for a long time. *My love for music.*

Adedoyin Ayeni

CHAPTER SIXTEEN

Damolà

Eleven Years Ago

My mum and I just moved to Nigeria. She said that we were here to start our lives afresh. I did

overhear her speaking to someone on the phone mentioning things like "It was time he met me and stayed with his family". I have no idea who she was talking to about on the phone but it seems like he was a major reason to why we were here. Nigeria was so different from New York. The climate was extremely hot and everywhere was so chaotic more than New York City.

We've been living in this flat ever since we arrived and it's not that bad. It's smaller than our house back in New York but mum said we would just be staying here for a little while and soon we'll be living in a really big mansion. I have no idea what she means by that because we had no mansion back in New York except she was planning to buy one over here in Nigeria. Living here hasn't been that bad and every morning I always wake up to this really beautiful tune and everyday I wondered where it came from exactly. Until I found out on one fateful morning on my way to school when I found this man at the back of the building holding a red acoustic guitar sitting on a wooden stool in just a white tank top and shorts. He looked so weird and out of place seated there but he didn't seem to mind it and in-fact reveled peacefully playing his music with a thin sheet of paper and pencil scrawled out on his lap.

His eyes finally caught me spying on him as he gave me a curious look wondering who I was before smiling me warmly at me.

"Hello and who might you be?" He asked nicely his deep scratchy voice making me feel a bit comfortable around him.

Who was this man?

"My name's Damolà" I said boldly coming to stand to right in front of him. He gave a smile to that dropping his guitar from his lap softly to the ground.

"It's very nice to meet you Damolà, I'm Olatunde." He introduced with an outstretched hand seeming very intriguing to me.

I took his hand shaking it the smile never leaving his face as he dropped my hand.

"I haven't seen your face before Damolà." He asked curiously.

"That's because my mum and I just moved here from New York" I answered.

His eyes seemed to light up in delight at that "Really? So you're the new neighbors?"

"Neighbor?" I asked confused.

"Yes my family lives upstairs" he pointed towards the steps that went upstairs.

I never thought anyone lived there though.

"I see. Why do you play your guitar over here then?" I asked curiously.

He chuckled to that before answering me "I'm so sorry son, my wife always complains that the sound of my guitar wakes everyone up too early and I mostly get my inspirations very early in the

morning. Since no one's lived downstairs in a while I decided to write my music here, I didn't think that the new neighbors had already moved in. I'll stop playing here, I wouldn't want to cause a disturbance to your family" he explained politely.

"Oh it's fine sir. We don't mind you playing your music here, I was just curious to see where the music that woke me up each morning was coming from." I answered.

He just nodded his head calmly at that giving me a thankful smile.

"You say your family lives upstairs right?" I asked as I watched him tune his guitar. "Yes. I have a daughter about your age." He answered.

"Oh, what's her name?"

"Daràsimi" he answered with so much pride in his eyes as he gave me a small smile.

That was the first time I ever heard her name and the time my love story with her started.

Adedoyin Ayeni